"W

he called sharply, r
head and facing the way it was pointing. "I know
you're there. If you don't come here, I'll send
Baylor after you!"

The threat was enough to send Robyn across the
sun-scorched beach to where they stood. She stared
apprehensively at the dog, restrained only by the
fingertips resting lightly on his head. It was with an
effort that she looked up at the man who stood
there, arrogantly assured, completely uncaring.

EDITH ST. GEORGE

is not only an accomplished writer but also a well-
known landscape artist. The varied settings of her
colorful fiction are as authentic and carefully drawn as
her spirited characters.

Dear Reader:

SILHOUETTE DESIRE is an exciting new line of contemporary romances from Silhouette Books. During the past year, many Silhouette readers have written in telling us what other types of stories they'd like to read from Silhouette, and we've kept these comments and suggestions in mind in developing SILHOUETTE DESIRE.

DESIREs feature all of the elements you like to see in a romance, plus a more sensual, provocative story. So if you want to experience all the excitement, passion and joy of falling in love, then SILHOUETTE DESIRE is for you.

Karen Solem
Editor-in-Chief
Silhouette Books

EDITH ST. GEORGE
Color My Dreams

Silhouette Desire

Published by Silhouette Books New York

America's Publisher of Contemporary Romance

SILHOUETTE BOOKS, a Division of Simon & Schuster, Inc.
1230 Avenue of the Americas, New York, N.Y. 10020

ISBN: 0-671-46961-4

First Silhouette Books printing March, 1984

10 9 8 7 6 5 4 3 2 1

To Robin K., who encourages, and willingly takes on the onerous tasks, setting me free to write.

With thanks.

1

Robyn moved the sculptured bronze horse a fraction of an inch on the glass and chrome cocktail table, bringing it into better balance with the low, ebony glass bowl filled with shaggy yellow chrysanthemums. She then checked the rest of her living room, feeling pleasure at its cool perfection.

The deep-piled carpet, sofa, chairs and walls were all white. Each accessory had been added only after careful consideration, from the tall blue Chinese jardiniere filled with bleached plumed pampas grass to the modern paintings with their bold slashes of color. The one-bedroom apartment, with its small balcony overlooking Griffith Park, was a showcase of sophistication and cosmopolitan taste, a perfect background for its owner.

Robyn checked the slim watch on her wrist before giving a final glance over the living room to make sure that everything was in perfect order. Each selection had been bought with Winslow's approval, and anticipation lit her dark blue-violet eyes. Winslow would be back today, and if he felt the same way he had on that last night before leaving, the evening could well end here.

"Lovely morning, Miss Stuart," the doorman said when she reached the starkly modern building that housed the Cornell Gallery in Los Angeles where she worked as the assistant director.

"Yes, isn't it," Robyn agreed, giving the sky an absent-minded glance. It wasn't her habit to notice the weather except to determine her choice of clothes. She was a city person, born and bred. A ride in the country held no appeal for her. It was just mileage to traverse in order to reach her destination. She'd created a lifestyle that satisfied her completely; there was no need to look further afield.

Before entering the gallery, she paused to run a manicured finger over her hip to smooth a threatening crease from the skirt of her oyster white wool dress. She touched the bib of fine gold chains to adjust their placement around the slightly shirred neckline.

It was a new dress bought especially for this day, and she checked her reflection in the display window. Her narrow waist was cinched by a wide brown suede belt with a square gold buckle. It gave accent to the proud lift of her breasts and the feminine flare of her hips. The full sleeves were fastened at the wrists with a row of square gold buttons. Winslow would approve, she knew. She looked polished and smooth, the chic cosmopolitan and, she thought, the perfect match to his urbane sophistication.

Certain that her makeup was faultless, she still reviewed her face with a quick glance. She was practiced at applying blusher to de-emphasize her somewhat square jawline, and the blue shadowing and kohl liner that accented her remarkable blue-violet eyes had been carefully drawn. Her nose was straight, with the suggestion of a tilt at its tip, and it needed only a light dusting of powder. Her lips, glossed in a color that matched her nails, were soft and full. The promise that lay dormant within their sensual curves had led more than one man to search for the passion they'd envisioned there—only to be disappointed.

Her tawny brown hair was streaked with gold, and she wore it short, with ruler-straight bangs across her forehead. She presented an immaculate appearance, a product of the lifestyle she'd created for herself.

"Good morning, Gretchen," she greeted the young receptionist as she entered the gallery. "I like that dress. Is it new?"

Gretchen struggled not to beam as she aligned the brochures on the current show's artists on her desk, but Robyn had already passed on to the office, her attention focused on the day's itinerary. Would Winslow come in this morning? she wondered. A slight smile touched her full lips, and she felt a tingle of anticipation.

It was her nature to move slowly, to evaluate all avenues carefully before reaching a decision. She was fastidious and selective, and at twenty-nine, she knew her mind. Winslow, before leaving for the South Pacific, had hinted at a closer relationship, and she'd decided it might be an enjoyable association. Their thoughts meshed at every level. Winslow lived for his gallery, and she was an art connoisseur. An affair with him would give them one more level for communication—a mutually pleasant one, she was certain.

That he was still a bachelor at forty-five and showed no desire to change the status quo would not be a problem. She herself saw no benefits to be derived from a marriage. She couldn't envision any man taking up space in her apartment. While she enjoyed socializing, her need for privacy was an essential part of her and jealously guarded. She was satisfied that Winslow felt much the same.

After seeing that his mail was sorted in neat stacks according to importance, she returned to the gallery to see that there'd be no jarring note to disturb him when he arrived. The main room was long and fairly narrow, but the angled partitions divided it into stalls where the work of individual artists could be hung for the best visual impact.

Winslow had always shown his appreciation for the smooth way she ran the business end of the gallery, as it gave him more freedom to do what he enjoyed most—searching out the gifted and still relatively unknown artists.

Winslow's taste and hard work had pushed the gallery to the top of the Los Angeles art scene—a position reflected in the quality of the paintings and sculptures. For an artist to be taken on by the Cornell Gallery was a mark of having arrived.

Winslow returned after she'd come back from lunch. Robyn was discussing an abstract painting with a potential customer when a soft ping alerted her that someone had entered the gallery. She turned to see him as he paused to answer Gretchen's greeting.

He looked up and caught her eye, then nodded slightly in acknowledgment, but he didn't approach. He'd never interfere with that first tentative interest being shown by a possible buyer.

Instead, he strolled around the gallery, and Robyn knew that by the time he reached his office he'd know from the number of replacements exactly how many articles they'd sold in his three-week absence.

From the corner of her eye she watched his progress, admiring the perfect cut of his charcoal suit, certain that he'd had it made while he'd been in the Philippines. Slender to the point of emaciation, he appeared taller than his five feet ten. His dark blond hair had some lighter streaks in it now, and he sported a light tan. He'd evidently found time to visit the beaches, and she wondered if it had been in the Philippines or Fiji.

Her gaze dropped to the leather portfolio he carried, and she felt a surge of anticipation. Had his trip to search out new artists been successful? The prospective client asked another question, and she reluctantly returned her attention to him. She completed the sale in record time, and finally was able to join Winslow in his office.

"I expected you here earlier," Robyn said casually, not wanting him to see she was piqued over not being called on his arrival.

He gave a fastidious shudder. "You wouldn't have wanted to see me. I looked and felt like a native. My first priority was to have a steam bath to make certain all the sand was out of my system, and then have Jacques cut my hair."

Robyn suppressed a smile. As far as Winslow was concerned, Jacques was the only hair stylist he'd ever consider going to. It must have been a strain for him to have gone three weeks without Jacques' attention.

"How successful were you?" Robyn finally asked.

"Not bad," he admitted. He unzipped the three sides of the large portfolio on his desk before unfolding it.

She could sense his suppressed excitement, and her interest grew.

"Were you able to talk Ramon Torquez into signing with you?" she asked, knowing that ever since seeing samples of Ramon's work in a brochure from a show in the Philippines, Winslow had been anxious to check further on the promising but little-known artist. Ramon had been the main reason for the trip. That, and an attempt to verify some exciting rumors from Fiji.

"Yes, and his work is as good as I had anticipated," Winslow reported with satisfaction. "We've agreed that I'm to have exclusive rights to show him here in the States. He has a dozen paintings that he's sending, so we should plan a show as soon as possible."

"And Fiji? Did you have any success there?"

His excitement grew as he bent over his desk and began removing the protective wrapping from what proved to be a square of canvas with careful reverence. "Turn around until I clip this to the easel," he ordered.

Robyn obeyed, amazed to note that his hands were trembling. Had the rumor brought back by a customer who'd seen a painting in a Fiji bar proven correct? Was Philip Holt cured and painting again? The art world would go wild to know that the superlative portrait artist was with them once more. Knowing Winslow's flair for the dramatic, Robyn waited patiently for him to finish, her back turned, an indulgent smile on her lips. How often had she seen him draw out the last bit of drama when presenting a painting to a client? As the tension grew, she admitted wryly, he was succeeding with her too.

"Now," he said, and she turned in anticipation.

Her first reaction was of surprise, then confusion. She'd been prepared to see a portrait, to admire the exquisite skin tones Philip Holt was famous for, and search for the inner soul of the subject, which he could depict with stinging accuracy if one was sensitive enough to see it.

Instead she was met with an onslaught of colors. They hit her, staggered her, and her arms crossed her chest in an unconscious shield against the emotions they aroused. The powerful colors ran rampant, a spiraling seduction that screamed for sensual release.

Never had a painting affected her so profoundly or with such intimacy. She felt naked, as if she'd been seduced and raped. No, never raped, she amended. She was reacting with a wild need to respond in kind, and she was shaken to her very core. She'd never experienced such a powerful reaction, and she felt momentarily disoriented, as if she'd been transported to another planet and had no point of reference as to how to proceed.

2

~~~ooooooooooo~~~

Robyn somehow managed to tear her eyes from the painting and meet the satisfied look on the face of the man beside her. She lowered her lashes, hoping desperately that Winslow hadn't been aware of the power of the emotions that had ripped so surprisingly through her.

Her eyes were drawn back as if by a magnet to the painting, but this time she was more aware of its power, and her expression was under control.

"Where did you find this artist?" Robyn asked enthusiastically. "This is stupendous! I hope you've been successful in signing him before he gets discovered."

"Look at the signature," Winslow said smugly.

She moved cautiously toward the painting, as if afraid it could reach out and pull her into its swirling depths. Annoyed by her reaction, she shook off the sensation and searched for the name.

The *P* and *H* were drawn in bold outline. It was a signature she'd seen many times, and she shook her head in disbelief. This dynamic painting had no relationship to the elegant yet frequently subtly damning portraits that Philip Holt was famous for.

"Who is he?" she asked, amazed by the anger she felt. Just because the man had tragically become blind was no reason for another artist to think he had the right to imitate Holt's distinctive signature.

"Yes, it's by Philip Holt," Winslow assured her.

She recalled the only time she had seen the artist two years before. A series of his portraits had been collected to tour the country, and she'd made a special trip to San Francisco to see it. As assistant director of the well-known Cornell Gallery, she'd rated an introduction and had been stunned on meeting him.

He stood six feet tall, and was overpoweringly masculine in his tuxedo. His dark brown hair curled where it touched his collar, and the trimmed beard and mustache were unable to hide the sensual sweep of his full lower lip. His equally dark brown eyes seemed to pierce through her, and under their onslaught she could understand the power they had to peel back his subjects' protective layers and provide such devastating insights into them.

He'd held her hand while focusing his attention on her, and she'd felt sympathy for the women who rumor said cluttered his life. What female could resist that intense concentration?

Someone tugged at his arm, and it was only then that she realized that the half-draped woman by his side was with him. Her mouth twisted in a wry smile. Was the rumor also true that he paid off his women with a portrait? Robyn could imagine what he'd do with this one, with her vacuous eyes and full pouting lips. He'd be unmerciful, but she'd never know it.

While viewing his work, she'd turned twice to find his eyes on her. Six months later, she read about his engagement to a wealthy society debutante, and she attributed the sadness that had clung to her the rest of the day to the fervent hope that it wouldn't interfere with his work. When the news that he was losing his sight shattered the art world, an ache enveloped her as she mourned with the rest.

"I managed to track him down on one of the off islands in Fiji, living the life of a recluse," Winslow explained, breaking into her reverie. "After seeing these spectacular paintings, I tried pressuring him into returning to civilization. The only reason he gave me this painting, I'm sure, was to get rid of me."

He paused, his mouth firming in a stubborn line as he stared fixedly at his assistant. "There were a stack of these piled in the back of the room. Once I show this, there'll be a line of art dealers heading to his island. But I saw them first, and I intend to have them. I'm sending you to get them, Robyn. I've booked a flight for you to leave in ten days."

Robyn looked at Winslow as if he'd grown horns. "What did you say?" she asked in disbelief. She loved traveling, but it was always to the art centers of the world, where she could be assured of the proper amenities—air-conditioned hotels, swimming pools and gourmet restaurants. Fiji brought forth pictures of grass skirts and thatched huts on sandy beaches, and she shuddered at the thought. "Why me?" she questioned.

"Because you're a very attractive woman, and Holt has been in isolation for a good two years," he said bluntly.

Robyn's head snapped up at his insinuation. "Just how do you mean that?" she demanded, her eyes blazing.

He flicked his long thin hand in dismissal. "Just what I said, and no more," he said sternly. "Surely you've heard about his reputation with women. For heaven's sake, I'm not expecting you to go to bed with him! But whatever abstinence he's had to practice should make him more susceptible to an attractive woman. As far as I could see, there were only a handful of natives on the island. He was the only white person there."

His gaze met hers firmly. "I've always appreciated your expertise as a salesperson, Robyn. You're subtle and convincing. Believe me, I tried my best to get Holt to agree, and I can only hope I softened him up a little. If it takes your femininity to further weaken him, I'll use it. I intend to be his dealer." His gaze shifted to fasten on the painting with a fierce hunger, and Robyn knew him well enough to know that nothing would dissuade him. Once that intense look came to his face, he would do everything he could to get what he desired. It came as a shock to realize that she'd seen that expression only over works of art, never a woman. And most definitely not over her.

The phone rang and he picked it up. When Robyn saw the conversation had absorbed his interest, she wandered out of the office, her anger still simmering over his intention to use her so callously, though she was honest enough to see his reasoning. She *was* an excellent salesperson, sensing instinctively how to convince a vacillating customer to buy.

She began to have doubts about establishing a closer liaison with Winslow, but then she stopped, distressed over her reaction. Why should she feel upset over the fact that possessing a painting meant more to him than a woman? The thought of any grand passion between them had never entered her mind. They were too in control of themselves to relate on that level.

Then she was reminded of her violent reaction to Holt's painting. She'd never responded with such depth of emotion to any person or object, had never suspected that she was even capable of the experience. For that searing minute, all her carefully nurtured sophistication had been stripped away and something deeply primitive had been in control.

It had been so alien to anything she'd ever felt before that she shied away from the memory, forcing herself to review her reaction analytically. She'd been susceptible because she'd been waiting for Winslow's return; she'd been caught off guard because she'd been expecting a portrait; she'd always reacted to the mixture of colors, and this was a spectacular rendition.

She accepted all the excuses, but knew none was the true answer. A tremor ran through her on recalling the magnificence of what she'd seen. She could appreciate the impact it must have made on Winslow, attuned as she was to the dynamics of abstract expressionism. What had his reaction been when he'd seen all of Holt's works? A sharp thrust of jealousy touched her because that opportunity hadn't been hers.

She smothered the desire to reexamine the painting, deciding to wait until she was ready to go home. Surely by then its force wouldn't overpower her, and she could examine it with a more dispassionate eye. The need to slay the dragon, to defuse her reaction, became a necessity. Her cool sophistication had been shaken, and she was wary of examining what it had exposed.

Robyn found herself uncomfortably haunted by the canvas. Forces seemed to be pulling her, urging her to come into its orbit for another, closer look. She found herself hovering near the reception desk at the front door, ignoring Gretchen's questioning glances as she moved with uncharacteristically nervous gestures to straighten an already straight frame, or dust a dust-free piece of sculpture.

This has to stop, she chastised herself in disgust, and when Winslow asked her to deliver a small piece of statuary that a client wished to keep on loan, she was only too happy for the opportunity to escape.

By the time she returned to the gallery, she was once again in control of herself. How could she have let a painting shake her so thoroughly? Yet, at the end of the day, when she went for the final examination that she'd promised herself, it came as a shock to discover that the easel was bare.

"Where is it?" she demanded, trying not to feel so upset by its absence.

"I took it to be framed," Winslow explained. He leaned back in his chair to look approvingly at her. "I've been so busy catching up with all the paper work, I never did say how lovely you look, my dear. Is that a new dress?" He paused, as if sensing her agitation. "Are you free this evening for dinner? You'll have to bring me up to date with what's happened while I was away, and I've got a lot to discuss with you."

He certainly did, she admitted wrathfully. He had been busy, and she hadn't wanted to disturb him, but if he thought she would agree to his outrageous request that she go to Fiji, he had another thought coming!

When Winslow arrived that evening, Robyn fixed a very dry martini the way he liked it—with a twist of fresh lemon peel. He was dressed with his usual elegant perfection in a dark brown suit and a pale yellow silk shirt with a subdued, patterned brown tie. Like her, he complemented the cool perfection of her apartment, and she felt slightly mollified.

Surely he didn't mean his outlandish demand. She'd been working with him for three years, and they were both fastidious and knew the other's abhorrence of the inconveniences they sometimes had to endure when pausing in unkempt villages to court a rising artist.

Fiji would be a catastrophe. She'd sensed his dislike when he mentioned the place, the revulsion over the thought of returning, and she knew that that was part of the reason he was wishing the trip on her.

She could sympathize with his feelings, so why couldn't he do the same for her? she thought rebelliously. Then she recalled the hungry expression on his face when he'd spoken of the remaining paintings he'd had to leave behind. A faint sigh escaped her.

By the time they returned to her apartment after dinner, she'd accepted the fact that she had her work cut out for her. Winslow abhorred controversial subjects while eating, so she'd remained silent, but now she prepared herself for the impending confrontation.

Winslow made it easier by bringing the subject up when they settled in her living room with large snifters of his favorite brandy. The dinner had been superlative, and he was in a mellow mood. "Don't forget to pack a bathing suit," he advised casually, while gently swirling the amber liquid before inhaling the rich aroma and taking an appreciative sip.

"Bathing suit!" she exclaimed in distaste. "You know I don't own one. I'm not what one would call a beach person."

He shifted his head, permitting his gaze to travel over her very adequate figure outlined by the clinging material of her black cocktail dress. "That's one of your more stunning dresses, my dear," he complimented her abstractly. "But back to the bathing suit. I didn't take one either, but there were a few times I wished I had. There's something about the blue water and the uncluttered beaches . . ."

Robyn looked at him in amazement. Was this *Winslow* speaking with that hint of longing? "Don't tell me the travel posters got to you!" she laughed mockingly.

"No, but it occurred to me that you really haven't had much of a vacation since you came to work for me. You could take some extra time there if you wish."

She wasn't being fooled. "You mean that Philip Holt may take more persuasion than you've intimated."

He had the grace to look embarrassed. "He seems to have settled into the native lifestyle, strange as it may seem, especially when one remembers how he was feted all over the world. Do you know how much one of his portraits was commanding before his sight started going?"

She'd heard, and astronomical as it was, she could believe it after having seen what he produced. There was no one that could touch him.

"I thought he'd gone into hiding because he couldn't paint anymore. Does he still have the master touch with the portraits you saw?" How terrible if he'd lost it!

"There were no portraits," Winslow confessed sadly. "I don't believe his eyesight is good enough to mix the delicate color nuances that he was famous for."

"How wonderful that he discovered this new style. His new work should make him just as famous."

"Yes," he agreed, "since by the nature of his disease, they'll be limited. While he never mentioned it, I have a feeling that his eyesight is still failing and there'll come a time in the not too distant future when he'll be totally blind."

Robyn absorbed his words in horror as a pain twisted through her. Again she recalled the tall, self-assured man she'd met in the art gallery that day. He'd been the reigning prince, holding the art world in the palm of his hand. What would a man of his caliber do when he could no longer paint?

An emotion welled up in Robyn, compounded of more than pity or sympathy—something she instinctively knew the man would have detested. Its force stunned her. She'd always been coolly in command of her feelings, unable to relate to the highs and lows that her friends suffered through.

She rose restlessly from her seat beside Winslow and walked to the window overlooking the park. She paused there, longing to be alone to sort out this unusual confusion.

"I know it's been a long day for you, Winslow, and I won't keep you any longer," she said, dismissing him. Forgotten was her intention to deepen their relationship this evening. She barely heard him agreeing with her before leaving. Her mind was on a lonely man on a lonely island, and the fear he must be battling each day as his eyesight dimmed.

There was no thought of arguing further about the proposed trip. She accepted, with a sense of fatality, that they were destined to meet. Hadn't the painting told her that the moment she'd first viewed _it_?

3

~~•oooooooooo•~~

Robyn finished the excellent New Zealand wine as she gazed out of the plane window, then fastened her seat belt as the plane dipped for landing. The Pacific lay calm and blue below her. She caught a glimpse of two fairly large mountainous islands with a spray of lesser satellites fanning out from them, which comprised the Fiji archipelago. Then the thump of the descending wheels warned that they were approaching the airport at Nadi.

It was late in the afternoon, but the heat overwhelmed her as she descended from the plane, making it momentarily difficult to breathe. By the time she collected her luggage and passed through customs, the promised air-conditioned room and bath rose to paramount importance.

She sat, steaming with annoyance at her perspiring discomfort, as the taxicab rattled to the hotel. The cab, admittedly, was clean, and the driver tiresomely cheerful, but out of necessity the windows were wide open to the breeze, and she could imagine what effect it was having on her usually immaculate appearance.

How in the world had she ever let herself be coerced into making this trip? she wondered morosely, not for the first time. Her mood had fluctuated widely during the past ten days from a suspenseful anticipation of succeeding in talking Philip Holt into returning, to wondering what type of fool she was to consider leaving the comforts of home for even this short period of time.

When she found Winslow uncharacteristically turning a deaf ear to her arguments, she consoled herself over the accolades she'd garner for returning Philip Holt to his rightful place in the art world. He might not be able to produce his superlative portraits anymore, but she was willing to wager that his present paintings would bring him even greater fame. He'd be a fool not to accept the glory and the limelight once again. After such a long abstinence, he must be hungering for the applause that had been his for so long. His many friends had treated him royally and would surely welcome him back. She recalled the proud way he carried his head, as if conscious of the crown he wore.

For the first time, she wondered about the woman he'd been engaged to and if she'd followed him into exile, but then recalled Winslow saying he was the only white person on the island. Had he broken that engagement when he discovered his eyesight was failing? She couldn't imagine any woman turning her back on such a vibrant, self-assured man.

She had selected the Mocambo Hotel because it

was near the airport, and since she expected to stay no longer than two days, it was ideal. It was surprisingly pleasant, but she was too exhausted to examine it. She'd just passed through several time zones, as well as crossed the international date line, and she felt out of synch.

The longed-for bath refreshed but also relaxed her, so that the bed looked too inviting to ignore. Deciding she wasn't up to spending the time needed to apply her makeup and dress in the usual impeccable detail she demanded of herself before going out in public, she had a tray sent to the room.

The next morning, Robyn felt rested and able to give her full attention to the problem of reaching the island where Philip Holt had exiled himself. Winslow had told her that it was called Yagatiki and was part of the Yasawa group. Her research had shown that scattering of islands curving like the thin tail of a dog off the northwest coast of Viti Levu, the main island, but Philip had chosen well. Yagatiki was evidently so inconsequential that it wasn't even named on the map. All she knew was that it was under a hundred miles from Nadi, and the small pontooned plane that Winslow had chartered to take him there and pick him up later in the afternoon had been relatively inexpensive.

It had taken him less than twelve hours to talk the artist out of a painting. If she went along with Winslow's usually astute evaluation of a person, Philip was ripe for further persuasion. Winslow wasn't one to send her off on a wild-goose chase. He must have had good reason to assume that she'd be successful in performing the coup de grace.

She was confident of her own ability to sway a doubtful client, knowing instinctively when to apply subtle pressure and when to retreat. Philip Holt, she was beginning to feel, was going to be her greatest challenge—and her greatest victory. She was excited at the prospect.

Winslow had already warned her that there was no place to stay on the tiny island, so she hoped her success would come quickly. She didn't relish having to make the trip too often in a small plane.

She had her usual breakfast of coffee and juice sent to the room. After a careful evaluation of an appropriate outfit, she decided her pale peach slacks suit in crush-proof polyester would be more practical for climbing in and out of a plane. If she found it necessary to utilize a more feminine armament for the next day, she could resort to the honey-colored silk shantung dress that did marvelous things for her ivory complexion and blue-violet eyes. Even though she realized Philip Holt might not be able to see the result, her makeup was applied with her usual meticulous care.

The man at the desk gave her his undivided and admiring attention when she asked who to contact to charter a plane. "Luvi is your man," he informed her with the wide smile she was becoming familiar with. "The harbor is too dangerous for a larger plane, and they don't have any landing strip." His dark brown eyes were full of questions. Why would so lovely a lady wish to go to such an out-of-the-way place?

Then, shrugging philosophically, he thought, Who could figure out the tourist?

Robyn's face was tight with surprise and annoyance when she hung up the phone after following his advice. Luvi, whoever he was, had told her his plane was out of service until a part was flown in from New Zealand, and he seemed unconcerned over the loss of a fare.

"When will that be?" she'd asked in dismay.

She could almost see the vague shrug. "When it arrives," he returned cheerfully. "Call me in a few days and we'll see."

A few days! Robyn fumed. She fully intended to be back in the comforts of civilization by then.

"The plane's not fixed as yet?" the desk man asked in sympathy.

It was evident that the island's grapevine was functioning, and Robyn wondered scathingly if it was done by tom-toms.

"Perhaps you can find a boat to charter at the docks," he offered helpfully. "I know none of the larger tour boats stop there. It's surrounded by a reef and only a smaller one can get in."

"I guess I'll have to," she agreed with reluctance, and, getting directions from him, she taxied to the quayside. She looked in dismay at the small boats still tied to the dock, then out to the blue water that lay between her and her destination.

The Pacific was not the serene ocean she'd seen when arriving the afternoon before. Whitecaps now crowned the building swells as far as she could see. No way would she trust her life in one of the boats that became increasingly smaller on inspection.

How did she ever get into this predicament? Robyn wondered crossly. The hot sunshine wasn't helping her temper either. There was a light wind blowing, but she was finding that her polyester suit, while ideal for being crease resistant, permitted little air circulation. It was beginning to feel like a plastic sweat suit.

Her attention was diverted by the squawking from a crate of chickens as a native carried it down the dock to a rusty-hulled tramp steamer tied at its end. The true Fijians, she was discovering, were tall, proud people and carried themselves with an innate grace. This one was dressed in faded jeans, his sweat-slicked upper torso accenting the bulging muscles as he carried his load with little apparent effort.

She moved into the meager shade offered by a palm tree while her gaze followed him with academic interest as she transformed the scene into a potential painting. He called cheerfully to several people chattering by the boat before going on board, and they hurriedly gathered bulging straw bags and followed him.

Robyn realized it was a ferry that evidently made its rounds of the islands, and it occurred to her that if she wished to get this job over in a hurry, this might be her only answer. While she eyed the boat with distaste, she admitted it was at least large enough to offer a sense of security against the waves that were rolling in over the beach with increasing determination.

She looked in vain for a ticket office before deciding the man watching the loading from the wheelhouse window was the person to approach. He wore a battered captain's hat. Robyn squared her shoulders, and she carefully made her way down the dock so the heels of her strapped sandals wouldn't catch in the spaces between the boards. Philip Holt had better be worth all this discomfort she was enduring for him!

The boat, she discovered with a refined flare of her nostrils, was not only in deplorable condition but was redolent with a mixture of odors that had her recoiling. The sun lay across her shoulders like a hot blanket, adding to the revulsion she was experiencing. She was shudderingly aware that beads of perspiration were forming on her forehead and upper lip, adding to her discomfort.

The need to retreat almost overwhelmed her, but the captain had been watching her approach, and he straightened when she stopped near the boat. His glance went over her indolently, and his smile showed his appreciation of what he saw.

"Can I help you, madame?" he asked with a heavy French accent.

Her determination to get to Holt's island permitted her to answer. "Do you stop at the Yasawa Islands?"

He stepped to the railing so his voice would carry over the bleating of the goats tied at the stern. "Yes, but there are several tour boats that go there as well," he answered, obviously regretful over losing so charming a passenger.

"I already inquired, but none stop at Yagatiki. Do you?" She was almost hopeful that his answer would be no.

He raised his eyebrows in surprise before pursing his lips and nodding slowly. "Whenever I have something—or someone—to drop off there."

She drew on her courage and suppressed her distaste of the dilapidated ship. She only hoped that

Winslow would appreciate what she was willing to suffer for him. "I need to get there today. Will you be able to take me?"

"Mais certainement!" he agreed. "But we have to leave in a few minutes. You won't have time to pack your luggage."

"I don't intend to take any." She considered it senseless since Winslow had informed her there were no hotels available. Besides, what possible need would she have for a change of clothes on a one-day trip?

His surprise was blanketed as he hurried to the gangplank to assist her gallantly on board. Robyn blanched as the earthy odors assailed her with new force, and his grin widened over her reaction.

"It can get quite overpowering," he admitted. "But come. You'll feel better with me up forward in the wheelhouse. There the breezes are blessedly fresh from across the sea." He ushered her past the curious but friendly glances of the natives sitting in what shade they could find, their possessions piled around them.

She went forward with him gratefully, and he dusted off a cracked leather bench, urging her to sit while he saw to the last of the loading. She took the opportunity to pat her face with a tissue and see to touching up her makeup. It had been through a grueling test, and she noted with satisfaction that somehow it had held up.

Fifteen minutes later she gratefully inhaled the promised fresh air as the boat pointed into the waves on its way to its first stop. By the time they unloaded at the second island, Robyn was fighting an increasing queasiness.

How far *was* the stupid island! she fretted. "How long does the trip take?" she asked irritably when the captain inched the freighter from the dock.

His shrug was a vague dismissal of time. "It depends upon how much cargo we have. The return trip usually is faster."

Thank heavens! she muttered silently, already thinking longingly of the cooling shower she intended to indulge in the moment she was back in the hotel later that day.

She was finding she was resenting with an increased passion everything about the passage. The boat was proving to be a tub that rolled and pitched with each wave, and the diesel exhaust was taking a demonic delight in blowing through the open windows and adding to her discomfort. She was barely able to tolerate the captain's ceaseless chatter as he probed unsubtly for the reason for her trip.

"The next stop is Yagatiki," he announced when under way again.

Her relief turned into a gag when one of the sailors brought in a tray with coffee and greasy donuts. She hadn't felt this miserable since her bout with the flu several years before. Scant attention was given to the islands as the boat wallowed by them. She was no nature lover, except when appreciating the way some artists had reproduced it. Besides, she was too miserable by now to notice how the clear air gave added brilliance to the remarkable colors of the water or the verdant islands.

She spent the last hour leaning back weakly in her chair, her eyes closed as she tried to tell her stomach to behave and not shame her. By the time the slowing of the engines alerted her that they were approaching her destination, she would have sold her soul for a bed and a cool shower.

Robyn was beyond reacting when she discovered that a tender was being lowered to take her to shore. Her hope for survival was pinned on reaching firm land. The reef surrounding the island, the captain explained as she paid her fare, prevented him from going in closer.

Past caring that the spray was drenching her, she clung in misery to the hard board seat as the sailor rowed carefully through a narrow gap in the reef and into the blessedly calm lagoon beyond. He beached the small boat and lifted her as if she were a child to carry her over the few remaining feet of water and deposit her on the sandy beach.

"The captain said he'll be back in two weeks to pick you up when he comes with provisions," he said, pushing the boat into deeper water before climbing on board and putting his back to the oars.

Robyn stood in appalled silence as the distance increased between them. Surely she had heard incorrectly! Much as she shuddered over making that ghastly trip again, it was impossible to consider staying even one night in this godforsaken place!

"Ni sa bula!" The deep mellow voice greeted her, and Robyn turned in surprise to find a small group of Fijians had gathered nearby, their dark brown eyes bright with curiosity, but their wide smiles a warm welcome. A tall, imposing gray-haired man, evidently the spokesman, repeated the greeting before waiting patiently for her reply.

It occurred to Robyn that they might not speak

English, and the enormity of that barrier was more than she could take in her exhausted state. "I wish to see Philip Holt," she enunciated slowly. "Is there a taxi—you know, auto—that I can hire to take me to him?"

The faces beamed, and she could have wept. They understood her! "Ah, our friend Philip," the old man said, nodding his head happily, his beautiful teeth flashing whitely against his brown face. "He lives on the other side of our island. But I'm afraid we own no car here. We have no use for one, and besides, there are no roads to drive it on."

He laughed, and everyone joined him as if it were a big joke they enjoyed sharing. Robyn managed to dredge up a wan smile to cover her dismay.

A slender girl, apparently in her late teens, stepped forward, her lovely face puckered in distress. "You've come to take Philip back?" she asked, her liquid brown eyes looking troubled. "Take that path," she said, pointing to a trail that led through a grove of coconut palms. "The path will lead you to his *bure.*"

The girl then hurried to one of the thatched huts that sat in the shade of several trees. It was obvious that she was upset over Robyn's arrival. Philip, it seemed, had not suffered his exile without certain benefits.

"You have no bags for us to carry for you?" the elderly spokesman asked in surprise, and Robyn was momentarily staggered. How was she going to survive with no change of clothes for the projected two weeks?

But Philip must have a two-way radio, she was

certain, and she realized she'd have to have him call for some assistance to get her off the island. This whole trip was proving a fiasco, and she was furious at Winslow. He'd never mentioned that there might be a possibility that she could be stranded in this isolated place. Winslow, she was discovering with newly opened eyes, had carefully deleted many pertinent facts when telling her about this trip.

"I'll manage," she said with a strained smile before starting on the shell-lined trail.

"I'll manage, all right!" she gritted through clenched teeth a half hour later. First she'd manage to throttle Winslow for insisting she come.

"You're a superb saleswoman," he'd snow-jobbed her. *"If you can't get him to return to civilization where he belongs, at least get his promise that I can have exclusive rights to his paintings."*

She paused to brace herself against a tree for the umpteenth time as she worked out a piece of broken shell that had lodged in her sandal. Winslow had talked as if their discussion would be over a glass of wine while sitting in Holt's air-conditioned living room. She fumed with rising anger. *"The path will lead you to his bure,"* the girl had said. From her studies, she knew that that was what they called their thatched huts.

Ten minutes later her anger had surrendered under her exhaustion. Her exquisite Italian sandals, which had carried her in comfort for hours in the gallery, offered no protection from the shell-and-coral path. The heat was intolerable, and the top of her head felt scorched even though she staggered from one tree-shaded area to the next, wondering over her increasing nausea. Her makeup, she was certain, had long ago melted to follow the rivulets of perspiration that ran down her cheeks and joined the stream that seemed to be forming between her breasts and down her back.

She'd thought she'd felt miserable on the boat, but now she was precariously close to collapsing.

Her suit had become a fiery armor, absorbing the sun's rays, and finally she could take no more. No one, not even the man who could use colors with such passion, was worth this torture! She stared dazedly around her, and for the first time realized she was skirting a lovely lagoon.

The water beckoned invitingly, and Robyn contemplated the bliss of walking into its cool depth until it reached her chin. Her heat-clouded mind was at first uncaring that she hadn't stopped to remove her clothes. It wasn't until the water lapped her knees that reason reasserted itself.

"No!" she gasped in horror. How could she, the cool sophisticate, have sunk this low? She staggered out of the water and looked aghast at her ruined shoes and wet slacks. With a trembling hand, she brushed at her hair hanging limply over her eyes, and only then noticed two black heads swimming in the lagoon.

She'd been so wrapped up in her private misery that she hadn't noticed them before. As she watched, they headed for the shore, and she started with surprise when she realized they weren't two people as she'd first thought. The large black Labrador dog came out about fifty yards from where she stood and shook itself energetically before turning to watch the man emerge.

He came out slowly, as if reluctant to leave the cooling water. His hair was long, touching his shoulders, and his features were hidden by his wet beard. His shoulders were broad, and as he emerged further, she saw the wide triangle of hair that covered his chest.

He stumbled, sinking into the water, and the dog gave a sharp bark. The man called to him reassuringly. When he stood up, his back was toward her. The dog barked again, and he turned toward the sound. Robyn sucked in a sharp breath as he strode to the beach.

He was nude, and for a moment the art connoisseur in her was transfixed by the magnificent body she was viewing. He was tanned a golden brown, and his muscles rippled in glistening highlights under the wet skin as he bent to stroke the dog with affection.

A breeze reached her, and she brushed at her obstructing bangs. The movement caught the dog's attention and he stopped his play immediately. A low growl rumbled warningly in his massive chest.

"Who's there?" the man called sharply, resting his hand on the dog's head and facing the way it was pointing. "I know you're there," he said more loudly when Robyn didn't answer. "If you don't come here, I'll send Baylor after you!"

The threat was enough to start Robyn across the sun-scorched beach to where they stood. She stared apprehensively at the dog, who was restrained only by the fingertips resting lightly on his head. He stood rock still, breathing growls in his chest, and it was with an effort that she looked up at the man who stood there, arrogantly self-assured and completely uncaring that he was still nude.

His hair was longer and his beard wasn't trimmed, but she knew that at last she had reached the end of what had become a test of endurance. Robyn felt herself sinking mindlessly into the sand at Philip Holt's feet.

4

~~~oooooooooooo~~~

Robyn heard the moan before she realized it had come from her. A cool damp cloth was being placed on her fevered brow and it felt wonderful. The sound of water splashing in a basin came to her as more cool cloths were placed on her chest.

A smile touched her lips as she felt the blessed relief. Her clothes, which had absorbed the heat until they became a hot box of torture, were gone, and her body could breathe once more.

She lay with her eyes closed, quiescent under the firm hands that removed the dampened cloths one by one to replace them with freshly cooled ones until her body was again covered by them. She wallowed in the relief they afforded, but with the relief, full consciousness returned.

Her eyes flew open, and she looked in startled

wonder around the room she was in. She was lying scant inches above the floor, but the mattress under her was comfortable enough. She'd never been inside a bure, but from the woven mats forming the walls, she realized that was where she must be.

Large sections were open to the elements, acting as windows, with mats rolled above them to be let down as shutters when needed. She saw through the openings that the thatched roof extended out to form a porch around the building, and that the room was surprisingly comfortable with the free-flowing breeze adding its relief to the shadowy interior.

A movement by the door caught her attention, and Philip Holt stepped into the room carrying a basin of water, his dog padding silently beside him. Remembering the effect his nude body had had on her, she breathed a silent sight of relief to see a short sulu fastened around his narrow hips.

Only then did it dawn on Robyn what had transpired after she'd fainted so ignominiously at his feet. He must have carried her here. A glance over her body showed he'd also undressed her before covering her with the relief-giving wet compresses.

The thought jerked her upright, the movement causing the pallet to rustle under her, and he turned to her.

"So, you've come back, have you?" he said coolly.

In spite of her embarrassment, Robyn's heart contracted momentarily when she saw his hand reach out to check the position of the table before placing the basin carefully on it. It was the act of a man who had to depend more on the sense of touch than of sight.

The cloths fell from her and she grabbed furiously for them. He seemed to sense her consternation, and the corners of his mouth turned in a bitter smile.

"You needn't fall apart," he said in derision. "I can only see you with any clarity in full sunlight. In here, you're an indistinct blur, so your modesty needn't be offended."

But you undressed me, she wanted to throw back at him, and her eyes dropped to the long slender hands resting on his hips. She wondered how much those sensitive fingers had relayed to him during the operation. In reflex, her arms folded over her high, full breasts.

"I don't suffer from false modesty," she returned pointedly. "But there was no need to undress me."

He gave a dismissive shrug. "Perhaps not, but you were suffering from heat stroke, even if it might have appealed to my male ego more to assume that the sight of me had caused you to faint. I thought it wisest to try and lower your temperature the quickest way available, whatever the cause."

Robyn struggled to come up with a cutting rejoinder, but the pounding in her head that had started when she had sat up was increasing, as was her nausea. It became imperative to lie down again before she embarrassed herself, and she collapsed with a groan.

He was by her side instantly, his hand on her forehead. "It's a miserable feeling, isn't it?" he said with surprising sympathy. "I know from experience. When I first came here, I didn't realize the power of the sun and had a touch of it also." His hand moved soothingly down her cheek and over her throat, pausing on the soft curve of her shoulder. "At least you feel cooler," he diagnosed clinically.

Too cool! she thought fuzzily a few minutes later, as the trembling that had started internally now set her teeth chattering. She was barely conscious of the wet cloths being snatched from her body and a cover being snugged around her. She was shivering uncontrollably, and she curled instinctively into the fetal position in an attempt to retain her remaining body heat. In her misery she despaired of ever feeling anything but this bone-chilling cold.

Suddenly she felt the cover being lifted from her back and a warm body pressing along its outline. "Relax, you poor kid," Philip breathed against the back of her head, as his arm encircled her to position her close to his long frame. "I've only the one blanket and I can see it's not enough. Let's see if I can help warm you a little better."

Robyn was beyond caring that only his thin sarong-like sulu separated their flesh. Her survival instincts had her pressing tight against him in her need for his body heat. The spasms slowly ceased, to be replaced by a yawning lassitude, and her lids closed in a healing sleep.

She awoke twice during the night, feeling abominably thirsty. Philip rose from her side both times, went outside and, after the sound of pounding, returned with a milky liquid that was coolly refreshing.

"What is it?" she asked after the second time. "It reminds me of something, but I can't place it."

"It's coconut milk, fresh from the nut," he informed

her. "I have no refrigeration here, but I've found it stays remarkably cool until I crack the nut open."

She felt a moment's revulsion over the primitive drink, but it had taken care of her thirst, permitting her to drift off to sleep again.

Robyn woke with the rising sun full upon her. Her eyes drifted open, then widened with alarm on seeing the bearded face a little more than a foot above hers as he stared down at her.

"You're very beautiful when you're asleep," he murmured, and she stilled her start of surprise, realizing that his only intention was to examine her now that the sun gave enough light.

She could imagine what she must look like with her straggly hair and no makeup. "That's very kind of you to say, but hard to believe after what I've been through the past twenty-four hours," she returned dryly.

He gave a dismissive shrug. "I'm not talking about the outside trappings. Your bone structure is excellent and your skin tone is exceptional."

He sounded so academic that a wry smile twisted her lips. So much for compliments. After all, he'd been a superb portrait artist and as such was conscious of details. "It's the first time I've been extolled for my bone structure," she muttered.

He shifted on his elbow as his glance lowered over the swell of her breasts, fractionally concealed by the thin blanket. "I can understand the reason," he admitted, a wicked smile curving the captivating mouth.

With him leaning over her at such short range,

Robyn was conscious of the changes the past two years had stamped on his face. The almost black hair was silvered with a light sprinkling of gray, but his mouth had the same remembered sensuous sweep and she moved quickly away from its disturbing promise.

The deep lines fanning from the corners of his dark eyes were new, telling of the squinting he must be forced to do to examine anything carefully.

Just how bad was his eyesight, she wondered, and was it getting worse? He evidently could see her up close and with the aid of the bright sunlight streaming through the door, but at what distance did she become blurred?

"Who are you?" he asked abruptly, breaking into her thoughts. "You evidently know me, but what brought you here?"

He seemed suddenly threatening as he shifted over her, intent on catching her expression. The action brought his hip against hers, and she became flamingly aware that neither one of them had any clothes on under the cover. When had he removed his sulu?

"I'm Robyn Stuart," she said in a strangled voice. "I'm from the Cornell Gallery. We met once two years ago in San Francisco."

He frowned, evidently trying to place the event. "You mean when I was coerced into making personal appearances when my paintings toured the country?" His abhorrence was evident, and she recalled wondering at the time if he'd resented being away from his painting.

"You wore a blue-violet dress, the same color as your eyes," he said suddenly, and she stared in

surprise that he should remember. "I've always reacted to color and it held my attention," he explained.
"You looked so cool and chic, yet the way your eyes
spoke and the way you walked . . . I found myself
intrigued and wondered which was the real you—the
facade you presented or the messages I was receiving.
I decided to wait until you finished looking around
before exploring the interesting possibilities, but you
somehow managed to escape me." His smile was an
outrageous seduction as he watched for her reaction.

She couldn't deny the thrill she was experiencing
over the fact that he'd remembered her, though she
doubted he'd been that interested. Still, he'd recalled
the color of her dress . . .

"You would have found it a little difficult with the
blonde fastened on your arm," she said with a small
moue of derision.

"I don't even recall her," he said dismissively.
"They were always matching me up with someone for
those openings." His hand dropped to her shoulder
and his finger began a sensitive search over the
hollows leading to her throat.

She was becoming shiveringly aware of the warmth
curling within her, an extension of the heat generating
from where their bodies had made contact. And now,
the light yet sensuous touch of his fingers combined
with the way her nerves were reacting to his devastating smile, stirring the growing warmth into an active
fire.

Her breathing grew agitated, causing her breasts to
make contact with the hair curling on his broad chest.
She flinched away and tried to hold her breath when
his glance shifted downward in full awareness.

His gaze drifted slowly upward again, resting momentarily on her slightly parted lips before meeting her eyes. An electric impulse flared between them, rendering her incapable of movement.

"So," he said, his voice lowering to a husky whisper, "we meet two years later . . ."

His head lowered slowly, and Robyn waited, the intense expectation an ache, until his lips parted to settle over hers. His mouth moved with a slow deliberateness as if intent on discovering every aspect of hers before starting on the next exploration. His tongue moved lingeringly along the beguiling curve of her lower lip until she became powerless to halt the invasion he was seeking.

Not that she wished to. New and exquisite sensations were curling through her, sensations she'd never before felt this intensely. She was conscious of a need to start her own explorations, and their tongues met and moved in a sensuous dance, a counterpoint of movements that left her breathless.

He tossed the cover aside as if impatient with anything that dared to interfere with his desire to discover every aspect of her body. His fingers were a searching, probing delight, every touch becoming a new revelation of the electrifying responses he seemed instinctively to know how to bring to fiery life.

"Philip, please . . . Oh, please, Philip," Robyn begged, her body quivering with its need for the ultimate fulfillment.

"Yes, my sweet sophisticated lady," he whispered in urgent response. But he anchored her hips so she couldn't hurry his tantalizingly erotic entrance.

"Now," he cried in challenge, and they moved with

an urgency that, when the final release came, had them collapsing in complete exhaustion, legs and arms entangled.

Robyn had no idea how long it took before she could again think coherently. In spite of the turbulence of what she'd just experienced, she was conscious of a deep inner peace, a contentment never before encountered. How could making love with this man have been so different? Whatever the reason for what had happened, she knew she longed to experience that magic again. She smiled drowsily and inched closer to the long body stretched beside her; her last memory before sleep was of his hand closing possessively over her breast.

The rich aroma of coffee awakened her and she stretched, at first aware only of her sated body, then opening her eyes as memory flooded her. Philip was by the two-burner kerosene stove, and her throat moved in an uncontrollable spasm on seeing him standing arrogantly nude, so completely unconscious of the power of his body.

Had that been the reason for her capitulation—the memory of the effect he'd made on her when she'd seen him emerging from the lagoon like some god cast in bronze?

She sat up abruptly, suspecting that that was only partly the answer but not wishing to delve further into what, for her, had been wholly out of character. She'd never permitted a man to go to bed with her before without long deliberation. What had happened was simply the result of her weakened condition after her heat stroke, and Philip had been despicable to take advantage of her.

She was surprised when the expected anger didn't emerge. Her innate honesty forced her to admit that she'd done nothing to dissuade him, had in fact encouraged him with a wanton abandonment that had amazed and, yes, fascinated her.

Where had the coolly chic art entrepreneur who had her orderly life moving smoothly disappeared? Somehow, ever since setting foot on these islands, that control had slipped from her grasp. What she needed to restore her to her accustomed equanimity was a shower, she decided. Philip had used sea water to cool her fevered body, she discovered as her fingers moved with distaste over the salty residue clinging to her skin.

As before, movement caused the soft crinkling of the filler in the mattress and brought Philip's attention to her. *"Ni sa yanira,* Robyn," he said, then translated the lilting Fijian greeting. "Good morning. I was wondering if you'd awaken soon. I hope you're as hungry as I am. In celebration, I'm sharing one of my remaining precious eggs with you."

In celebration of what—her easy capitulation? she wondered stingingly, but was momentarily distracted by the effect of his disarming white-toothed smile.

"I would prefer to have a shower first," she said stiffly, annoyed at having allowed his smile to affect her so easily. His casual unconcern over his nudity must be getting to her, but it wasn't as if she'd never seen a man undressed before. The fact that his bronzed body looked like a pastiche of the best features from all the famous statues of Greek gods she'd ever viewed shouldn't make such a difference.

Her mind might utter the warning, but she was

finding it took a major effort to tear her fascinated gaze from him as he stood before her with easy nonchalance. The fact that his body was completely tanned with no hint of white lines showed how far he'd slipped into his role as a native.

For the first time, Robyn began to hold serious doubts about the successful outcome of her trip. This was no man brooding in enforced exile, but a vital person who had met and accepted the challenge of his adopted environment.

"Shower? What's that?" he responded with an easy laugh. "Fresh water, you'll discover, is something we hoard very carefully on this island. You'll learn to accept the slightly astringent feeling that salt leaves on your body, though I admit to running outside with a cake of soap in hand whenever it rains!"

Her mouth curled in distaste at such primitive living. She'd never sink so low. But what was she thinking of? She'd be away from all this in a few hours, as soon as he made contact with Nadi. "I guess I'll have to wait until I return to my hotel. Will you please phone or radio for someone to come for me? I know this island is off the usual route, but I'm willing to pay the going price."

Philip stood with legs spaced, his fists on his hips, as he looked at her with aggressive amusement. "Look around you, my dear innocent. Do you see any radio, or any sign of a telephone? There's no electricity or even a generator on the whole island. That's one feature I checked out thoroughly before I chose to live here. Unless you've already made prior arrangements, I'm afraid you're stuck here until the supply boat returns. It stops here about every three or four weeks. If they broke their routine for you, it was only because you made it worthwhile."

A cry of dismay escaped before Robyn could stop it. She'd thought the fare high, but had felt too miserable to care about anything but the need to get off the boat. But to think she was marooned here for two weeks was more than she could tolerate.

"The hotel! All my luggage is there; I brought nothing along. Surely if I don't return, they'll alert the police to see where I could have disappeared to!"

"Did you tell them you were coming here?"

She shook her head, then realized that with the sun no longer sending its bright beams into the room he probably couldn't see the movement. "No, but they knew I was trying to find transportation here," she said with rising hope. "When I couldn't get a plane, they suggested I try to charter a boat."

"That's your answer then," he said with a casual shrug. "They'll figure you were successful and will hold your luggage until your return, so you needn't worry about losing it. They've long since become used to the odd capriciousness of tourists. Experience has taught them not to start being concerned until at least a month has passed."

"I don't believe you!" she gasped, even as she suspected with a sagging feeling that his evaluation of the situation was accurate. She hugged herself in sudden fright as the full extent of her plight washed over her. She had plenty of traveler's checks in her pocketbook, but what good were they on an island that had no hotel, or even stores, as far as she could see? She'd never felt so helpless, so out of control, in her life. "But what can I do?" she said in a taut whisper.

Philip reached for two mugs and filled them from the coffeepot. "You drink this first," he said, handing one to her. "Then I'll show you the path to the . . . facilities. When you return we'll have our breakfast, and then I think a swim will be in order. After that, I get to my paintings. As for you . . ." He gave a faint shrug. "There's a whole island to explore."

His voice was firm, and for once Robyn permitted someone else to take over the reins for the moment, admittedly too bewildered by the turnabout to offer any objections. Besides, the coffee tasted like nectar in her dehydrated state.

Sense was returning with the reviving drink. Philip had joined her, sitting at the foot of the bed, and she was discovering his apparent unconcern over their shared nudity was more than she could take. He was sitting too close. By reaching out, she could touch him, and the desire to do so grew at an appalling rate.

Fully awake now, she remembered too vividly how the muscles banding his back had felt under her hands, how the friction of his chest hair over her sensitized breasts had thrilled her. Such wanton behavior was beyond anything she'd done in the past, and she attributed it to her weakened state. "May I have my clothes?" she asked stiffly, banishing the intruding memories.

"Surely you don't intend to wear that suit again?" he reprimanded. "I felt the heat that came from you when I peeled it off. Were you intending to kill yourself? Cotton is the best material in the tropics."

She hitched the cover more securely under her arms. "And meanwhile, what do I wear—this blanket?" she taunted.

The remembered wicked smile lit his face. "Why wear anything? I'd like to introduce you to the wonderful sense of freedom not wearing clothes allows." He angled his head, his expression sardonic. "Do I embarrass you with my nudity?"

The question was huskily seductive, and Robyn instantly backed away from its power. She'd succumbed once, but she was in full possession of her faculties now. "I'd prefer it if you wore something," she admitted tightly.

His chuckle held pure devilment, but he rose and went to a woven basket in one corner. "I guess I'll have to indoctrinate you slowly," he said softly with an exaggerated sigh that brought angry spots of color to her cheeks. She had never considered herself a prude and didn't appreciate being ridiculed as one.

He drew out a gaily patterned rectangle of cloth and fastened it around his lean hips. It was a sulu, she recalled, and imagined that it was a practical and cool garment. She'd seen men wear them in various lengths from the ankle to above the knee. Philip, unfortunately for her newly sensitized nerves, wore the shorter version that did little to hide the muscular thrust of his thighs.

He brought two of the garments to her. "I guess you need more coverage than I do," he said with mocking solemnity. "These will have to do until Serina comes. Maybe she'll have an extra dress she can loan you."

"Serina?" she asked, as she struggled to fasten the first one around her breasts before standing to fix the other one around her hips. They were meant for his narrow waist and hips, and not for her more curvaceous shape. She had to resort to using pins dug from her pocketbook.

"There's only one place to land on this island," he said. "Surely Pappa Nia and his family were there to greet you?"

She recalled the stately elderly man and suddenly realized that except for a few of the younger boys, he'd been the only male, even though she'd seen half a dozen huts. "Don't tell me they practice polygamy here!" she cried in outrage. In her dazed state, she'd been vaguely aware that two of the women had appeared to be pregnant.

He looked at her in surprise; then, realizing her assumption, he threw his head back with a roar of laughter. "Pappa Nia is man enough and would enjoy the inference." His face then became sober and he explained further. "Selina is his granddaughter. The other women are here under his protection while their assorted husbands go to the other islands to try and make enough money to support their families. Two men are in New Zealand, and their wives are lucky if they see them once a year. They're all waiting patiently until their husbands can afford to have them come live with them. The women try to help, and go periodically to see if there's work in the various resorts, but with the economy . . ."

He needed to explain no further. Robyn could feel a twinge of sympathy for the unfortunate couples, but she recalled the faint antagonism of the lovely dark-eyed girl when she'd asked how to contact Philip Holt. She was certain she was Serina.

Robyn looked at Philip, who was now back at the stove. Two years would be a long time to be without a woman. Having read descriptions of the easygoing nature of the islanders, she was certain he'd not been deprived of that amenity. She viewed with distaste ever wearing one of the woman's gowns, vowing to make do with what Philip had to offer until she could leave this place.

Robyn shrank with horror when she discovered, after following a short path, that the facilities Philip had promised consisted of a seat over a hole in the ground, with a shovel on the pile of sand next to it. How much further would she have to sink before being rescued from this prison? she thought in disgust.

All too aware of his amusement when she returned, she hid behind a stoic front, knowing he'd been prepared for a burst of outraged protest. She'd trained herself well over the years. There'd been many mini-catastrophes that she'd handled at the gallery without becoming the least ruffled. Artists, she'd discovered, were prima donnas where their paintings were concerned, and buyers could be just as demanding. She'd been proud of her ability to stay calm, and she drew on that same pride to help her cope with the present difficult situation she found herself in. Somehow she'd survive, especially now that she suspected he fully expected her to cave in under the trying days ahead.

He had breakfast ready, and when she said that all she had was juice and coffee, he brushed her protest away brusquely. "I have only two meals a day, so you'd better learn to eat when you can. When I'm painting, I have no time to stop to consider food."

The mango was sweet and tasty. She ate the perfectly cooked three-minute egg, remembering the warning about their rarity. Robyn was surprised by her hunger until she realized that, except for the coffee and orange juice the morning before, she hadn't eaten anything.

"You'll have to dunk the bread," Philip said as he nonchalantly broke a crisp piece from the loaf and dipped it into his mug of coffee. "This is baked on the island and dries out quickly, and I found that this is the only way to eat it."

Robyn's lip curled, shuddering over what to her was the height of bad manners. She caught the glint of mocking amusement in his eyes and wondered if his sight were as poor as he'd indicated or whether he could pick up the vibrations from the people around him, as many similarly afflicted persons were known to do. His portraits had shown a great sensitivity, and she wouldn't be surprised if that ability was helping him cope with his blindness.

"It just occurred to me why Serina hasn't been here yet with a fresh loaf," he continued conversationally, while breaking off another piece to offer to her. "She usually comes twice a week to check on things and clean up a bit, but she must have seen you and is staying politely away." He leaned back in the chair and his lips parted in the smile she was finding so disturbing. "I suspect the natives have a well-developed sixth sense. It wouldn't have done for her to come upon us earlier, would it?"

Her coffee mug was slammed on the table in anger. How dare he laugh at something that had been so special to her! She felt abused and lashed out at him in retaliation for the hurt. "I think you're despicable! Don't think I have to stay around and be laughed at!"

Her chair crashed back as she pushed away from the table to storm away from his taunting presence. His hand shot out to stop her flight and grazed her shoulder. It gave direction to his other hand, and he grasped her arm.

"Wait, Robyn, don't fly off like that," he begged in an odd voice that made her eyes flash up to examine him. "I didn't mean that the way you took it."

His expression held fleeting pain, a vulnerability that startled her, and she found herself unable to offer a further rebuff when his hands captured both her arms. "It looks like I've forgotten how to act with a lady." His mouth moved in a wry twist of self-condemnation. "The few times I've gone to Nadi, the company I met at the bar had less class than what I'd usually traveled with in the past. Which doesn't excuse me, I know, but shall we start fresh? I was going to ask you if you'd join me in my morning swim."

He was holding her close as he strained to see her in the shadowy room. A new sensation flooded her: deep compassion for the man who had stood proudly at the top of his profession, only to be cut down through no fault of his own, and who was now struggling to create a new life for himself.

"I'd like that," she agreed in a more controlled voice.

"Great!" he grinned with relief and gave her a swift hug before clasping her hand firmly in his and leading her from the thatched hut.

Baylor, who had been lying quietly next to the door, rose with a happy wag of his tail to cavort around them as they dashed across the sun-heated sand. Philip stopped her at the edge of the lagoon, the water lapping gently at their feet.

"We've used up my supply of clothes," he warned. "I have only two changes besides what I'm wearing, and you're using both of them. I advise you to remove them, otherwise you might find the dried-on salt can be very chafing." He'd already untied the material around his waist and tossed it out of the surf's reach.

I wish he wouldn't do that! Robyn groaned inwardly, even as she watched with hungry excitement as his bronzed body arced in a dive and met the small wave sliding to the beach.

Baylor gave a joyful anticipatory bark before joining his master, and Robyn hesitated only a moment before she nervously unpinned the two pieces of material. Already the sun was hot on her body, and she was yearning for the promised refreshment offered by the crystal-clear water.

Where was the woman who'd coolly dismissed Winston's suggestion to take along a bathing suit? she mused in silent wonder short minutes later. She didn't know how to swim, but she was discovering the warm water sliding over her skin to be a very sensually pleasant feeling. No wonder skinny-dipping was so popular, she thought.

As each wave lapped lovingly against her body, it seemed to wash away another layer of the controlled reserve she'd so carefully built around her over the years. She was conscious of a sense of release, an awareness of the heightened receptivity of her flesh, which had been so flamingly brought to life short hours before.

Robyn watched with amusement as the two dark heads swam the length of the lagoon and back again. The waves lifted her gently, and she found herself enjoying the sense of momentary weightlessness they gave.

The dreamy contentment returned to enfold her, different from and yet seemingly a part of what she'd experienced after their lovemaking.

The two dark heads finally turned to the shore as they had the day before when she'd come upon them unexpectedly. She realized with a tightening around her heart that Philip must be depending upon Baylor to lead him back to safety. The black Labrador shook the water from himself, but Philip, after flicking his thick hair from his face, turned back to the sea, and with head cocked in a listening position, he finally called to her. "Robyn? You better come out before you become a prune."

"I'm coming," she answered quickly, surprised at how the tight sensation in her chest had become a knot on hearing the uncertainty in his voice. He couldn't see her, had no way of knowing if she were still in the water!

She left the water and came swiftly to him in a need to reassure him that she was there. "I've never cared for bathing at the beach, but I confess to wishing now that I could swim. You make it look like fun."

His hand went out to rest on her arm. "I could teach you. It isn't difficult, especially with the buoyancy this water gives you."

"I'd like that," she admitted, and was surprised that it was true. Winslow would never believe she'd ever said that! Winslow would never believe this whole series of events, she amended, and for the first time realized that he'd be expecting to hear from her, certainly in a day or two. What would he do when that call didn't come?

"What's the matter?" Philip asked, and she realized he must have felt her muscles tighten under his hand. How sensitive he must be, to pick up her concern. She was inches away from the vibrant naked body of the man she'd just made love to, and thoughts of Winslow were an intrusion.

"Nothing," she returned, trying not to notice the tremor passing through her.

But Philip had evidently sensed it, and his free hand went to grasp her other arm, brushing over her breast in the process. Robyn was stunned by the tingling shock wave that spread from the point of contact. They were standing close enough so that he could see her clearly with the bright sun shining full on her face. Their eyes locked, and Robyn saw his brown eyes darken to become almost black as his long sensitive fingers rested lightly over the rounded shape of her breast before slowly cupping it as if needing to test its weight.

Her nipple became taut with an aching swiftness, as if it were already programmed by the sweet memory of the adoration it had received short hours ago. "Philip." It was an urgent whisper on her lips, which she was unaware of saying.

"Yes," he answered her plea, his grasp firming over her breast as he pulled her close. "Yes, Robyn," he breathed, before his mouth settled in possession over hers.

A flame started deep within her, building with

incredible speed. She was consumed with the need to have him share the conflagration, only to discover he was scorching her with his own fire. They sank to the sand, and there, with an occasional wave reaching out to lap at their feet, Philip reaffirmed the pleasure that his kisses could give. The heat they generated soon had their bodies crying to be melded into one.

Robyn had never felt so exquisitely alive. The breeze was an added caress over her wet body, the sun a heated kiss. The sand rubbed fingertips of awareness over her sensitized skin until Philip's added weight drove her into the warm hollow they were creating with the force of their lovemaking.

They climbed together steadily until they shot into outer space, there to shatter into small fragments before slowly gathering the pieces into a whole again as they floated back to earth.

"Come," he whispered when their breathing quieted enough to permit speech. He took her hand and raised her on shaking legs to lead her into the gentle swell of the water.

At first it felt icy on her heated skin, but then it refreshed her. But the water's relaxing properties were lost as Philip gently washed away the sand clinging to her body. When satisfied that she was free of the sand, he cupped her face and placed a tender kiss on her mouth. She followed him in bemused compliance when he again took her hand and led her from the water. They paused to permit her to scoop up the discarded clothing before returning to the hut.

"You're some lady," he whispered huskily, gathering her close as they lay on the mattress. His kiss was gentle, though she was aware of the fires that for the moment were safely banked. "It's a little late to remember how sick you were last night," he said ruefully as he tucked her close to his side. "But you should be resting today."

"Mmm," Robyn agreed drowsily, too lethargic to say more. She buried her face in the warm curve of his neck to place a kiss there. Her last thought was of how delicious she found the salty flavor of his skin.

5

∘૭૭૭ᐭᐭᐭᐭᐭᐭᐭᐭ૭ᐭᐭ∘

Robyn stretched, wondering why her muscles felt stiff, and became wide awake as memory flooded back. Philip was an ardent and demanding lover, expecting as much as he gave. She remembered the bite of the sand on her back under the weight of his hard body. At the time it had acted as an added stimulation to her sensitized skin, but now she ruefully admitted to wishing for the skin lotion sitting in her hotel room in Nadi.

She reached out her hand and turned her head at the same time and became aware of the void beside her. The room was empty, and she stared at the indentation on the pillow for long minutes, wishing that the dark head was still there with a stark longing that frightened her.

The intense feeling bewildered her. She'd never felt

this way over a man before, and she stood up quickly to banish the disturbing intrusion. What was it about this island, this man, that had geared her emotions into such a pitch?

She shook her head as if by that action she could cast out all the incredible happenings of the past twenty-four hours and return to her usual calm, assertive control. How had she ever permitted Philip Holt, a comparative stranger, to seduce her not once, but twice? she chastised herself with growing anger. Needing to regain her former poise, she refused to permit herself to remember her own uninhibited responses. Her lip curled in self-disgust over her capitulation.

An unreasoning need to castigate herself arose, feeding her anger. It was easy to extend that anger to include Philip for having so easily shaken the very foundation of her carefully structured life. She looked around in distaste at the few pieces of crude furniture, the bare minimum of equipment in the kitchen area. When her gaze fell on the faded pieces of material that were supposed to clothe her, her disgust found an outlet.

The fact that she'd been in a weakened condition from seasickness and later heat prostration was no reason to have lost control of herself as she had done. Philip Holt might be content to live and act like a native, but she was again in control of her faculties. Though trapped into remaining here for two weeks, she'd show him that she, at least, was too strong willed to revert to the level of the natives, even if he had.

Her rebellion had her searching for the clothes she'd

arrived in. She finally found them draped over a line strung between two posts on the back porch. Her nylon panty hose were beyond redemption, but the suit proved worthy of the label that promised it to be wrinkle proof. She felt a sense of deep satisfaction when she was once again dressed properly, and she looked with disdain at the two pieces of material that had done little to hide her curves. How could one remember to act civilized when dressed like that?

It occurred to her that if she could talk Philip into wearing at least jeans and a shirt, he might become more amenable to remembering what he'd given up in committing himself to this exile. After seeing his painting, she was convinced he owed it to the world as well as to himself to return to his rightful position as one of his generation's most brilliant artists.

Robyn brushed her hair with violent strokes until it fell into its usual sophisticated flip across her forehead. With only the small compact mirror for guidance, she applied her makeup with care. After a final check of her suit, she raised her chin with determination.

She was once again in command of herself. Winslow had sent her on a mission, and she had every intention of bringing it to a satisfactory conclusion. Whatever had caused her aberration, it was behind her and to be forgotten. If she failed in convincing Philip Holt to return, she would at least get his promise to send his paintings to the Cornell Gallery.

But where was he? she wondered. The slant of the shadows of the palm trees on the sandy beach showed she'd slept a good part of the day away, and she felt better for it. She left the protection of the bure and blinked in the still-bright sunlight. The heat blanketed her immediately, and for a wavering second she wondered if seeking the protective barrier her elegant suit afforded her was a very smart idea.

Robyn glanced back at the inviting shade offered by the thatched hut. She could now understand why the four sides were kept open. Any vagrant breeze seemed to find a home there, and it had been remarkably pleasant in its shadowed interior.

A movement further along the beach caught her attention, causing her to squint against the sun's glare. It was Philip. He was standing in the shadow cast by a tree, but his easel was in full sun. He had stepped back to get a better view of his painting and the movement had caught her eye.

When she was halfway to him she wondered if she'd lost her mind, plowing through the soft sand under the still-hot sun. She was disgustedly aware that under the airtight armor that her suit had once more become, small rivulets of perspiration were starting between her breasts, and her carefully applied make-up was melting away. Her once-beautiful sandals added to her discomfort. There was no use in dumping out the sand. They'd fill again with the next step.

By the time Robyn reached Philip her irritation had risen in proportion to her blood pressure. What sins was she paying for, to be placed in this abominable situation?

Baylor, who had been resting in the deeper shade offered by a clump of bushes, came to her when she stopped in the shade behind Philip, and the dog placed a large, damp and sandy paw on her trouser leg. Robyn didn't pause to consider if it was as a greeting or a warning not to disturb his master; to her it was the last straw.

"Get away from me, you beast!" Robyn cried, jumping back as she brushed furiously at the clinging sand. To her horror, tears coursed down her cheeks. She hated putting on less than fresh clothes, and seeing the further destruction of this, her only garment for the duration of her forced stay, was her breaking point. Her nerves, already drawn to their limit from struggling to come to terms with the strange environment, had to seek release. She found herself crying, something she couldn't remember doing since childhood, and it further demolished her composure.

Philip turned. "What's going on?" he demanded.

"Nothing's going on," Robyn snapped. "I'm just being attacked by this monster."

He laughed. "Baylor wouldn't hurt a fly unless I told him to. He was just warning you not to disturb me."

His smug laugh added fuel to her resentment. "Oh, pardon me. I didn't know that I had to first make an appointment. You should have informed me about my error before, when . . . when . . ." Oh, Lord, how did one stop these tears from pouring out?

"Robyn?" Philip peered at her in perturbed surprise on hearing the betraying quiver in her voice. He placed his palette and brush on the collapsible table by his side and reached out for her.

"Come closer so I can see you," he urged. "I left you sleeping, looking like an angel, and now there're tears . . ."

Already ashamed of her outburst, Robyn had no intention of obeying, but she found her head cradled against his shoulder. One sensitive hand massaged muscles tightened into knots at her neck while the other stroked soothingly along the curve of her back. It was impossible to prevent her body from relaxing against the firm strength of his. But suddenly she was pushed roughly from him.

"What in the world is the matter with you?" he cried in evident annoyance as he tugged at her sleeve. "What kind of fool are you, insisting on wearing these clothes? Wasn't one touch of heat stroke enough for you?"

Robyn's reaction was predictable. She was in no mood for his recriminations. That she was sweltering under her suit, proving the truth of his words, only made her more incensed.

"Though I'm trapped here, it doesn't mean I have to sink to the heathen level that some people seem to have done," Robyn returned in biting sarcasm. "I'm certain this Serina, who seems to be taking such good care of you, must have a decent dress that she'll let me *buy* from her. Until then, I prefer to act like a civilized person!"

Her tirade brought danger signals to his eyes. "And to think I had forgotten what snobs I had escaped from," he snapped, his lips curling in disgust. "If you feel that strongly about our way of life, how did you ever agree to lower yourself by coming here? I certainly didn't issue any invitation." He paused, and by the way his expression tightened, she knew he'd found his own solution.

"That was dense of me, wasn't it?" he said. "I should have known giving that painting to Cornell to get rid of him wouldn't satisfy him. He had to send his number one assistant to try and seduce the rest of the canvases from me. I've always dealt with Marshall in San Francisco, and I have no desire to change."

He thrust his face closer to hers so that there'd be no doubt about the extent of his scorn. "Too bad you played your cards all wrong, honey. Weren't you supposed to have kept your body to barter with until I was panting so hard I'd promise anything? Well, I tasted what you have to offer, and while I found the merchandise acceptable, do you think you were really *that* good? You must know what price I can claim for my canvases, and believe me, I'd never pay that amount to any woman!"

Robyn was momentarily stunned by his attack; then a burning ball of rage started deep within her, growing into an explosive force. Merchandise? . . . Acceptable? The words hung in midair between them, outlined in crimson flames. The contemptible, egotistical lowlife! she blazed inwardly, her fury making speech impossible.

Her hand flew upward but stopped inches from his face as she realized in horror what he had almost driven her to do. She'd never felt the need to resort to violence; but then, she'd never been flayed so unjustly as this before. It took superhuman willpower to return her hand to her side, and her nails cut half-moons into her palms.

"What's the matter, did I hit too close to the truth?" he asked with a short mirthless laugh.

Her body trembled under the leash she just barely managed to clamp on the fury struggling to erupt. "If I were a man, I'd beat you senseless!" she ground out, biting her lip, hating the giveaway quiver in her voice.

70

She wouldn't cry; there was no reason to! She wouldn't allow any man, and certainly not this—this *animal,* to tear away the cool control that she'd been so proud of for all these years.

But she realized it would take only one more derogatory remark and she'd be reduced to screaming epithets at him. He was beneath contempt, but she conceded that distance was necessary if she were to hold on to her self-respect. No one, especially not this miserable excuse for a man, was going to reduce her to act the harridan! With self-preservation her primary goal, she turned and fled.

6

As she ran, the loose sand tugged at her feet until, gasping painfully from the unaccustomed exertion, Robyn paused and glared over her shoulder at the man responsible for her chaotic state of mind.

Philip was standing with feet spread and fists on his hips as he stared out over the lagoon. Anger was expressed in every taut line of his body. As she watched, he unfastened his sulu and, casting it aside, ran down to the water. Baylor looked at him quizzically, then jumped up to run protectively at his side.

The sun shone full on his canvas, drawing her eye, and even at that distance Robyn could see the tremendous sweep of colors. It brought her to a full stop. The fury drained from her as if a stopper had been pulled. She'd been too highly trained as an art connoisseur for too many years, and her body tingled with a new force at what she saw.

Philip's first painting had been a powerful display of leashed passion that had torn great rents in her controlled sophistication. This one, while not finished, was a jubilant exultation of the spirit, singing with the joy of a Hallelujah chorus.

Robyn had worked too long, had stroked too many sensitive and easily bruised egos of various artists not to know how difficult it was for them to return to a special mood once it had been disrupted, and she was aghast at what she had done. What irreparable damage had she done by shattering Philip's concentration at this critical moment of creativity? She might feel threatened by being thrust into this alien environment, but it was unforgivable to intrude on the genius of this man.

Robyn pushed her hair from her heat-flushed face and stared around her in a half-dazed state. The cumulative effects of the past two days had her feeling completely drained. She'd gone through more physical and emotional battering in that time than during her entire adult life. It became imperative to find a place to rest, and though she flinched at the thought of returning to Philip's home, there was nowhere else to go.

The sun was again proving to be an enemy. Her head was pounding, and at that moment, the lowly pallet held more allure than the satin-sheeted bed in her exquisitely appointed apartment. By the time Robyn staggered into the cool interior of the hut, her head was aching so badly she could scarcely see. She barely managed to struggle out of the doubleknit suit that had precipitated the confrontation with Philip. She groped blindly through her pocketbook for the necessary aspirin before collapsing on the bed.

Perhaps Philip was right, she conceded in weary defeat. It would be wiser to save the suit until she could leave. She'd never survive if she insisted on wearing it daily. As it was, it was in pretty bad shape, and she shuddered, thinking of the picture she'd present on the return trip before reaching the hotel and her luggage. Winslow, how could you have done this to me? she moaned before sleep claimed her.

The rich smell of hot coffee woke her. Robyn's eyes slitted open and her gaze rested on the shadowed figure working by the stove. Philip's hand went to the shelf above it and slid searchingly along its edge before removing a can. It wasn't until later that she discovered the notches carved in the wood telling the location of the cans of meats, vegetables and fruits. But at this time, seeing the groping hand, she was caught unprepared by the aching spasm claiming her heart on observing the evidence of his encroaching blindness.

Robyn made herself remain still even though her impulse was to aid him. After all, Philip had been preparing his meals without help for a long time. It wasn't pity or sympathy that she felt—she sensed he'd hate being on the receiving end of those emotions—it was more of a maternal feeling. She realized she wanted to help ease his way as he went down that lonely path to total darkness.

The interpretation startled her. No one, certainly not a man, had ever brought forth that emotion in her, and she pulled away from the thought. Fool! she berated herself. She was nothing to him, and once free of the prison the island had become, her only contact would be the paintings Winslow hoped she'd persuade him into sending.

She frowned as thoughts of her employer rose in her mind. Had Philip, more knowledgeable of the male mind, been correct in interpreting Winslow's reasoning in sending her here? In fact, hadn't she accused Winslow of basically the same thing? Knowing of the intense hunts conducted by all galleries to find and acquire top artists, it was reasonable that anyone as astute as Philip would believe it of them.

Was that why she had run from Philip? Had she backed away because she knew there was more than a grain of truth in his accusation? Not that she'd ever stooped to using such tactics, but she knew with sudden clarity that Winslow wouldn't object to whatever lengths she went to as long as the paintings came to him.

The nap had cleared her mind, and Robyn could now sympathize with Philip's reasoning even as she agonized over it. Those two spontaneous acts of love had been so special to her, and the idea that he thought of them as advance payment for goods she hoped to receive tore at her so that she had to press her hand against her abdomen to still the turmoil.

The movement caused the mattress to rustle, and Philip's head cocked in her direction. "Awake?" he asked. "Supper will be ready as soon as I open some of these cans and get things heated."

His voice held no remnants of his earlier anger. The swim must have done for him what the necessary sleep had for her—given them each time to rethink the recriminations they'd thrown at each other. They were trapped into having to live with each other for the next two weeks, and she prayed that he'd softened in his conviction about her tactics so they could live in reasonable harmony. She couldn't bear another confrontation like the one they'd had that afternoon.

She'd always carefully avoided any intense emotional stress because she found it too upsetting. Yet here, in one day with this man, she'd been torn apart, experiencing the emotional high of the total giving of love followed by the degrading low caused by the demeaning epithets they'd thrown at each other.

"I'll set the table," she returned in a satisfyingly even tone, while reaching for the two pieces of material which would comprise her wardrobe for the coming days. If he was willing to call a truce, she was mature enough to comply. Nothing would be gained by keeping up a running confrontation. For all intents and purposes, they were alone on the island. She was completely out of her element, reduced to relying on him for direction on even the basics of this primitive living. There was no telephone to lift to order anything, no store to go to for essentials, and she shuddered in distaste over the level she was being reduced to exist in for the duration.

They ate in a neutral silence. The canned stew caused Robyn's nose to twitch in dislike, but she found she was too hungry to refuse it. Her last decent meal seemed to have been eons ago. As she looked at the utilitarian stainless steel utensils and heavy crockery, memories flitted through her mind of the gourmet meals she usually enjoyed with candlelight, snowy linen and sparkling crystal and silver.

The bure, bathed in the transient afterglow of the

sunset, gave barely enough light to see what she was eating. Didn't Philip at least have candles? she thought with irritation, but that quickly faded after seeing him grope for the mug of coffee by his plate.

A sharp growled oath erupted when the cup was jostled and the hot coffee just missed burning his retreating hand. "Why the devil don't you put the mug where it belongs?" he growled, reaching with assurance and placing it in the correct position.

"I'm sorry," Robyn managed stiffly. "I'll be more careful next time."

"It would help," he muttered, and for the first time she heard the bitterness in his voice, giving her an inkling of what he'd been forced to endure, the massive reeducation that he'd had to undergo to reach this level of self-sufficiency.

As the light faded, she realized Philip must be almost totally blind. Candles would be useless to him. The thought caused her throat to constrict, and she, too, groped for her mug. In the deepening darkness, she missed, and a sense of frustrated helplessness hit her. It struck her that this must be what Philip had to face all the time.

Robyn drew in a sharp breath as a deep compassion swept through her, stilling her hand. Following on its heels came a surprising anger. Where was the woman he'd been engaged to? She should be by his side, giving him the comfort and encouragement of her love. He shouldn't be alone to face the terrible uncertainties that lay in his not-too-distant future.

As independent as he seemed, the catastrophe that had befallen him could eventually crush even a man of his strength, especially when total blindness occurred.

What would he do to express himself when his brush was forever stilled?

Robyn had never before experienced a compassion so deep. It was almost an ache. She felt apprehensive over the new and disturbing sensations she was experiencing since coming to this island.

Though Philip's face was now indistinct, his features were clearly imprinted in her mind. But it was not the rather scruffy beard and overlong hair she saw. Instead, it was the smartly trimmed man she'd first seen two years before. Had he really remembered her as he'd stated—was it only that morning? Doubt rose, but he'd recalled the color of her dress, and the thought brought forth a strange warmth in her.

"I'll do the dishes," she offered when they finished.

"Fine," he agreed. "I'll get a pail of fresh water for you."

Robyn's mouth twisted in wry humor over his quick acceptance. How like a man to happily hand over the kitchen cleanup! Still, as long as she had to stay, it was only fair to do her part of the chores. In fact, if she took on all the household duties, he'd have more time to work at his painting. She was conscious of an uncomfortable sense of urgency, as if time were slipping by too rapidly. As if the time were near when the shutters would be closed forever and his life as an artist would be over.

A despondency settled on her and she struggled to shake it off before Philip returned. There was nothing she could do to stem what was in his future, and she couldn't understand why she was reacting so sensitively to his silent suffering. The evidence demonstrated that he was managing to carry the cross by himself. Why then was she being teased with this desire to ease its weight a little? She'd kissed and been kissed by other men, had felt their passion, but none had invaded her inner and deeply buried sensitive nature.

She was glad to turn away from her unusual introspection when Philip returned with the bucket of crystal-clear water from the lagoon and poured some in the wash basin sitting outside on a bench.

Was that what he washed the dishes in? Robyn shrank from the thought, recalling pictures of the microscopic plankton and other wriggling creatures that lived in sea water.

Robyn sucked in a fortifying breath. "Where's the soap?" she asked in a strained voice.

"I don't use any. All you get are curds in salt water," he explained nonchalantly. "If anything sticks, I use some sand. Here, let me show you."

He reached for a rough rag hanging on a nail hammered into the beam supporting the overhang. He scrubbed a plate in the basin, then rinsed it by dipping it in the bucket. "Simple, isn't it?" he commented, handing her the cleaned dish.

She took the plate and, unconsciously imitating him, ran her hand over it, testing its cleanliness. "It seems so," she admitted, remembering with a sigh her fastidious scalding of her lovely china at home.

The moon wasn't up as yet, but the star-crowded sky gave an amazing amount of light. Robyn bent to her self-imposed task, glowering after Philip's figure as he disappeared down the beach, the black Labrador a dark shadow by his side. The least he could do was stay and dry, she muttered in irritation as she slid a hand over the plate's surface, testing its cleanliness to make certain she was as thorough as he'd been.

Her irritation increased when she looked for a towel. It was now completely dark inside the room, and she muttered several explicit epithets when she barked her shin on the chair she'd left pushed out from the table. Philip, she recalled, had returned his carefully under the table, and she wondered how many bruises he'd suffered before he'd memorized the placement of each piece of furniture. Thoughtfully, she returned hers before shuffling across the floor until she reached the bed.

She sat on its edge, pushing her hand disconsolately through her hair. How was she going to survive? she wondered in despair. Her watch was in her pocketbook, but she guessed it was close to nine. If she were home in civilization, she'd be dining with a considerate escort in a subdued but elegant air-conditioned restaurant, served by attentive waiters. Instead, she was sweltering in the unaccustomed heat and had eaten canned stew and—she shuddered—had been reduced to washing dishes in cold sea water!

An insect buzzed by her face and she swallowed a scream. How dare Philip go off and leave her sitting in the darkness to be attacked by what could be poisonous insects! She bit her lip in apprehension, her ears straining to hear if Philip was returning. In the ensuing silence, she became aware for the first time of the myriad of strange noises coming from the thick forest behind the hut.

To her city-attuned ears, the clicking beetles and the shrilling crickets sounded as if they were gathering forces to attack. A branch crashed down somewhere in the woods and she shivered anew. What man-eating creatures inhabited the forbidding woodland? she wondered wildly.

When a dark shape loomed in the doorway, she was too terror stricken to cry out. It bent over as if to leap, and she froze, unable to move.

"Sleeping inside or out, Baylor?" Philip murmured softly as he scratched the dog affectionately behind the ear, and the air rushed from Robyn's lungs as she collapsed against the pillow in reaction.

Philip cocked his head, alert to the telltale sounds from the mattress. "In bed already? Good. I'm sorry that the night life here is so limited, but I'll do my best to supply the entertainment."

Robyn leaped from the bed as if scorched. Despite the darkness, she could sense the mocking leer in his smile. The uneasy truce was evidently over. "You're out of your mind if you think you're going to spend the night in bed with me!" she said coldly. Did he think two weeks of "entertainment" was due him as payment for room and board?

"Aren't you forgetting something?" His voice floated, silken soft in the darkness, but Robyn was not fooled. There was granite underneath the thin veneer, hard and unyielding. "There's only one bed, and having become an uncivilized native as you've accused, you're lucky I don't demand you sleep at its foot on the floor."

"You don't have to be insulting!" she snapped.

"I'm only trying to live up to your expectations."

He moved, and for a disconcerting minute, Robyn lost him in the darkness. In the ensuing silence, the cacophony from the insects swelled threateningly in the night air. "Philip?" The small cry was an urgent appeal for reassurance.

"Yes?" The answer came unexpectedly from the other side of the bed.

"Don't sneak around like that!" she cried, her painfully frayed nerves driving her close to hysteria. "Aren't there any lights in this godforsaken place? Just because you can see in the dark doesn't mean others can!" She stopped, aghast at her cruel words.

There was a long painful silence, broken by the sound of Philip moving away from the bed. Robyn stood, shivering, waiting for retribution. She jumped again on hearing a metallic sound and located Philip by the stove. There was a rasp of a match, and in its sudden flare, she saw him light a candle and place it in a wooden holder. An open tin canister sat on the table, exposing a further supply.

"I'm sorry. I should have told you where they were kept. I have no use for them and forget that others do." His voice was empty of all expression, but Robyn flinched, sensing the underlying bitterness. How could she have been so thoughtless! "Another reason for not using them is that the light attracts insects."

Robyn found herself by the table. She took a deep breath to steady her voice. "Then we'd better not leave it lit," she said, bending over and blowing it out. She took another, smaller breath. "Which side of the bed do you prefer?" She had a craven need to pull the cover over her head until she'd sorted out her confusion. How could she detest this man for his biting words, yet feel such compassion for him?

"It makes no difference," he returned.

And it didn't, she found out shortly. The bed was slightly wider than twin size, but Philip managed to take up the larger portion, making no concessions for her. She clung defensively to the edge, her back to him, but her muscles soon protested at the strain. In spite of her long nap, she had hoped for the swift release of sleep.

Robyn's lips twisted in wry acceptance. Who was she kidding? She was flamingly aware of every move Philip made as he settled for the night. He respected the space she was struggling to keep between them, and made no effort to touch her. Yet the warmth of his body was enveloping her like a caress, and her imagination was giving her no peace.

Pictures flashed of him emerging from the lagoon, unconcerned with his nudity. Again she marveled at the perfection of his bronzed body, and her fingers twitched in reflex as she recalled how the muscles along his back had felt under her questing hands. How could his body fit so perfectly to hers? There had been a oneness in their lovemaking that defied description.

Her muscles were soon screaming to relax from the taut hold she had on them, but she lay balancing at the edge of the bed until his slow, even breathing indicated he was asleep. Only then did she ease carefully onto her back, to be immediately caught up in a flash of intense heat. Her hand had inadvertently brushed his hip, and the warm smooth skin alerted her that, unlike her, he'd removed his sulu. Instant recall inundated her with how his hard, forceful body had transported her.

She was beaded with perspiration. At work, at home, everyplace she went she'd lived in a climate-

controlled environment. Now she found that the
breeze that usually swept in from the sea was nonex-
istent, and the heat became unbearable. She refused
to accept the possibility that a large part of her
discomfort was caused by the man lying beside
her.

Her desire for a cooling shower became an obsession, and perversely, knowing it was impossible, the
need became more imperative. The only relief could
be found in the lagoon, but she shrank from the idea
of going to it. Even the thought of crossing the short
strip of sand in the dark made her shiver.

The room became suddenly lighter, and she turned
startled eyes to the doorway. Robyn caught her breath
at the magnificent full moon as it seemed to rise out of
the ocean. The moonlight shimmering across the
lagoon was a beckoning path, urging her to follow it.

Philip moved beside her, and her gaze turned
toward him to find that he'd merely shifted position.
The arm that had lain between them was now resting
over his head. In the process, the thin blanket had
been tossed aside, so that only a token corner covered
his middle.

Robyn couldn't stop her gaze from sliding over his
exposed form. His long muscular legs extended to the
bottom of the mattress, and her examination drifted
upward as she feasted her eyes on the perfection of his
body. She followed the shadowy triangle of hair over
his chest, pausing to admire how swimming had
developed his pectoral muscles. She watched the even
rise and fall of his breathing for long minutes before
moving on to examine the features of his face.

But here she was thwarted. Though his face was turned toward her, the heavy beard and mustache created shadows that blurred its conformation. She was swept by an almost uncontrollable desire to place her head on the shoulder exposed so invitingly, to slide her fingers through the silken roughness of hair covering his chest until every curve, every band of muscle was programmed in her fingertips. Then to explore further . . .

Appalled by her thoughts, she found herself standing in the middle of the room, knowing that she needed to get away from the temptation. There was only one way to neutralize the heat coursing through her body, and she took flight, all concern for what could be awaiting her outside the shelter blanked out by the need to reach the cooling water.

She didn't stop until the wavelets lapped at her ankles and she was faced with a new apprehension. What dangers lurked under the deceptively silvered lagoon? Content in her insular way of life, she had only marginal knowledge of what she could expect. Strangely, when she'd been with Philip she'd felt no fear, but she lacked the courage now to go further on her own.

But she still felt the need to cool off. Surely nothing could attack her at the water's edge! Drawing consolation from the thought, she undid the two pieces of material and tossed them up on the beach. Settling on her knees, she scooped up what water she could as each wave reached her and splashed the water over her heated body. It was far from satisfying, but it was the best she could do under the circumstances.

"So this is where you disappeared to."

Robyn rose swiftly, a startled cry on her lips. Philip stood behind her, the faithful Baylor by his side. She closed her eyes in a defensive reflex, but her lids became a screen, reproducing in minute detail the magnificence of his bronzed body, silvered in high relief by the moonlight. Oh, Lord, couldn't he have had the decency to put on his sulu? she wailed inwardly.

"It was too hot. I couldn't sleep," she muttered, her gaze fastened safely on the black dog. The moonlight glinted off Baylor's tongue as he panted softly. She grimaced in disgust. Even the animal looked like he was leering! Only then did she realize that she, too, was completely nude. How much was Philip able to see in this bright moonlight? she wondered, as she searched for the place she'd tossed her coverings.

"Then why don't you go in for a swim to get the full benefit?"

Robyn glanced over her shoulder at the lagoon and shivered. "And get eaten by a shark? I have more sense than that!" Her voice was shrill from her effort to suppress the emotions his appearance had triggered in her.

"I should have explained this lagoon is safe. That's why I had my place built here. There's an inner reef that stretches across the mouth so that the larger fish can't come inside. Now that I'm here, I'll have a swim too." He took a step into the lagoon, then paused. "But I forgot—you don't know how to swim, do you? Come, I'll stay with you. Between Baylor and myself, you'll be safe."

He extended his hand, and Robyn found hers placed in it. His long, slender fingers closed reassuringly, and as if triggered by some strange alchemy, her apprehension disappeared. Nothing, she was positive, could harm her as long as he was by her side.

The water felt deliciously refreshing as they waded in until Philip stopped. "How deep is it on you?" he asked solicitously, his free hand going to her shoulder. Finding it well above water, he slid slowly down her arm, pausing for a long minute when the back of his hand brushed the soft curve of her breast. The water lapped caressingly over her suddenly sensitized skin, and she caught her breath at the strength of the reaction that coursed through her.

"It's deep enough," she returned, hoping her voice didn't reflect the tremors attacking her. What moonlight madness was affecting her? she chastised herself. She was no teenager, new to the touch of a man's hand. After all, he couldn't see her, she reasoned, and had to orient himself by touch and sound.

"Can you float?" he asked, and when she confessed she couldn't even do that, he stepped behind her, his hands cupping the sides of her head. "Lean into me," he directed, "and let yourself relax. Your natural buoyancy will do the rest. Don't be afraid. I'll keep your head above water," he reassured her when he felt her body tense.

She couldn't tell him that it wasn't fear that caused her reaction, but the realization that if this contact was prolonged, she could well find herself over her head figuratively as well as literally.

"Trust me," he murmured in her ear. His head was

bent to hers, and as his beard brushed her cheek, all her vacillation slipped away and she gave herself into his keeping.

Robyn had always carefully thought out the pros and cons of every step she'd taken, but for some reason her mind and her body were in rebellion against her old practices. When his hand slid down her back to her waist to give added support, she lost herself in the unsuspected delight of the waves surging caressingly with a sensuous enchantment over her bared flesh. The water's movement washed her floating body lightly against his and pulled it away in a tantalizing rhythm that succeeded in teasing her senses into a voluptuous awareness.

"You're doing well," he said encouragingly. "Now move your arms and feet."

She did as directed and felt a moment of loss when his hands slowly withdrew their support, but she was soon too involved in keeping herself afloat to feel any alarm. Philip was pacing alongside her, and she heard the soft plopping sounds of Baylor swimming on the other side.

How had he managed to eradicate her fear? she marveled, as her eyes drifted languidly skyward to find that only the brighter stars were able to compete with the light cast by the full moon. Yes, this must be moon madness, she admitted dreamily—a madness that was somehow peeling away her layers of inhibition.

A larger wave washed over her and she sank beneath the water in sudden fright. Strong hands reached for her, and she was pulled, sputtering, against Philip's chest.

"I'm sorry. I should have warned you about those rogue waves. I've been hit by them often enough," he apologized, and held her against him while giving a few therapeutic slaps to her back as she coughed to regain her breath.

She brushed her hair from her face and looked accusingly at him. Her hand stilled as she became aware of his body pressing against hers, and the words forming to castigate him died in her throat. She tried to resurrect her anger as a shield, but the emotion dissipated before she could give it substance. The surging water was playing its teasing magic on her again, bringing them together and pulling them apart in an erotic simulation of the love act. Her fingers trembled as she touched his face, brushing aside the strand of hair clinging wetly to his forehead.

"Robyn." Her name was a husky sigh as he cupped her head.

She waited in breathless fascination as he slowly lowered his head. His lips covered hers and a soft sigh escaped. This was what she had been wanting, what had driven her from the bed. She'd been a fool to think she wanted to escape this exquisite devastation.

7

The meeting of their water-slick bodies was a new sensation. She'd fled to the sea, seeking its cool relief, but now the flames he was so adept at igniting canceled its aid. She was burning out of control by the time he released her mouth.

"Come," he whispered huskily into her ear as he took nerve-jerking nips at the lobe. "I'm too old to practice my skills in the ocean."

The moon highlighted the roguish smile on his lips as he took her hand to pull her from the surging water. "And we're bypassing the beach, also. We, my dear witch, are going straight back to that bed you left so precipitously."

She heard the chuckle rumble deep in his chest, and couldn't help joining him. Had she ever felt so wonderfully alive, so delightfully unfettered? It was as if a camouflaging cloak worn too long had been thrown aside. If this was moon madness, she'd take a large dose of it!

They paused at the water's edge to indulge their need to touch, to see if their kisses were really so intoxicating. "Vixen, witch, siren from the sea," Philip growled into her mouth in between fiery kisses. "You'd better take me to the house this instant or suffer the consequences."

A moment of deep compassion intruded through the joyful haze that enveloped her. Without Baylor's aid, Philip had no idea which direction to go. Sensitive to his pride, she took his hand and teasingly urged him into running with her up the short incline. They arrived breathless and laughing, but once inside the bure she was pulled back into his arms.

She raised eager lips to him and his kiss surprised her with its infinite tenderness. Where before his kisses had burned her with demanding desire, she now experienced an unsuspected gentleness, a sweet giving that brought momentary tears to her eyes.

He drew her to the bed and lowered himself beside her. The fierce urgency that had driven him before was gone. His hands were featherlight as they traced their way over her body, molding, gliding, touching with sensitive thoroughness. Every part of her was explored with a reverence that had her quivering with an unexplainable desire to cry from the power of the emotions he evoked. No man had ever been able to make her feel this pride in her body; no one had ever truly awakened her femininity.

"You're so beautiful, so beautiful," he murmured

huskily when he cupped her face, his questing hands stilled for the moment.

She sensed that his perceptive artist's hands had taken over the duty that his eyes could no longer be relied upon to fulfill. But now she needed his kiss, and her fingers moved over his still-damp hair, pulling his head to hers.

He responded at once to her urgency. The time for tender exploration was over. He'd found all her sensitive areas, and now he put the information to use with erotic stroking and nipping love bites until she was moaning his name while writhing in exquisite need.

Her hands darted over his body in urgent forays until his frenzy matched hers and he rose above her to settle in the nest of her thighs. They reached the summit in quantum jumps, there to leap into the unknown darkness. Slowly, hearing only the thundering ovation of their hearts, they drifted back to reality, clasped protectively in the security of each other's arms. No words were spoken. There was no need for any when Philip placed a final soothing kiss on her love-bruised lips before rolling on his side. She was pulled close, her soft curves molded to fit the muscular angles of his body.

Robyn drifted awake to a new dawn and stretched, conscious only of a wonderful surfeited feeling. Memory returned on hearing the clatter of dishes—memory of a night with no comparison.

Philip! Her hand reached out automatically, and she discovered that the space beside her was empty; then she recalled the sound that had awakened her. She sat up quickly, driven by an urgent need to reassure herself that he was still there.

Philip was by the stove, filling the coffeepot from the covered bucket of fresh water sitting on the small work table. He'd informed her the day before that he filled it from a small creek which flowed a short distance behind the house. It didn't occur to her that she wasn't shuddering in disgust over the thought of utilizing untreated water as she'd done the day before.

Robyn realized that she wanted to know more about this fascinating man, wanted to find out how he'd learned to cope in this strange environment and what his innermost thoughts were about the catastrophe that had cut him down at the height of his fame. True, his new paintings would add to his stature, but time was working against him. When his sight failed completely, what then?

Robyn quickly buried her despondent thoughts. Fate had decreed that she be marooned here for two weeks. After that she doubted she'd ever see Philip again. She'd seen enough of the man to know that Winslow had been a fool to think that she or any other person could influence Philip to do other than what he wished. He'd selected this island as his retreat for reasons of his own. Who was she to try to lure him from this haven he'd created?

The rising sun was flooding the inside of the bure with light, but she was learning his habits and knew from the cock of his head that it was his acute hearing that had alerted him that she was awake. Robyn also saw that he was again without clothes, but this time she accepted with a calm equanimity the unabashed exposure of his magnificent bronzed body. This was evidently the norm for him and she had learned her lesson. She was the intruder into his world. Who was she to tell him how to disport himself?

"The coffee won't be ready for another five minutes," Philip informed her.

"That should give me time to brush my teeth," Robyn answered, tossing aside the cover. Only then did she remember that the two pieces of material that she depended upon to cover her were still somewhere on the beach. Well, she decided philosophically, if he could traipse around in his birthday suit, so could she. She walked with what she hoped was acceptable nonchalance out into the sunshine.

"I hope Serina comes today. This is the last of the bread, such as it is," Philip commented later over breakfast as he dunked a dried-out slice into his coffee.

Robyn fished a piece out of her mug. Dunking, she was discovering, was an art. If immersed too long, the soaked piece was apt to disintegrate and fall away. "What time does she usually come?" she asked, her gaze going to the two pieces of material drying over the line on the back porch. They'd been damp and sandy when she'd found them, and she'd waded into the lagoon to rinse them clean. She hoped they'd be dry enough before the girl arrived.

Upon returning, Robyn had been thankful to find that Philip had put on his sulu, and she'd slipped on the camisole top she'd worn under her blouse. Unfortunately, the eyelet-laced whimsy ended just below the curve of her hips and her flesh-colored bikini pants were scant covering. Still, they helped her face the man across from her with more composure.

"She usually arrives later in the morning after they finish baking," Philip informed her. "She comes twice a week with supplies and takes care of whatever has to be done around the place."

Robyn topped their coffee cups, surprised at her building resentment over the imminent invasion of their privacy. There was no reason why she couldn't take care of whatever had to be done. A frown marred her forehead as she realized the possessive pattern of her thoughts. But, she quickly rationalized, her daily schedule had always been crowded, and she suspected enforced idleness would soon drive her crazy.

She glanced at her empty wrist and gave a sigh of frustration. "I wonder what time it is? The battery *would* pick this time to run out!" she said, her voice showing her vexation. She'd discovered the evening before that her watch had stopped, and it had seemed a catastrophe. Her life had been programmed by the hours and minutes, and even now, with nothing pressing to be done, she felt at a loss.

"What difference does it make?" Philip asked with what evidently was hard-learned tolerance. "You'll find that here time puts pressure on no one. The sun comes up and it's a new day. When it goes down, it's time to go to bed." He gave her a wicked smile before continuing. "One learns the hours, the minutes are unnecessary, something contrived by man. One's hunger tells when it's time to eat, or thirst when it's time to drink."

Yesterday that philosophy would have brought forth a terse rebuttal, but today her body and her mind were replete after a night of love, permitting her to smile indulgently. Her eyes became heavy with memories as her gaze rested on the man sitting across from her. Then they slid to his hands resting on the table. Those long slender fingers had held such magic. . . .

Rising quickly, she gathered the dishes and took them outside to the wash bench. She paused to gaze at the picture made by the sandy beach sloping to the small protected lagoon. Last night the moon had laid a magical silver path across the water. Today the lagoon held a new allure: an expanse of diamond-dusted wavelets beckoning her to come and enjoy its pleasures. The evening before she'd sought relief for her heated flesh. She'd discovered that the cool water could do only so much, that the bed that she'd fled from had given her her ultimate relief.

A gust of wind rattling the palm fronds sounded disconcertingly like rain. "Do you see any heavy clouds?" Philip asked, and Robyn glanced to the doorway where he stood, squinting into the sunlight as he tried to see what he was searching for.

Compassion tightened Robyn's chest but she was careful to keep it from showing. She glanced up at the palms now swaying gently. "I don't see any. I guess it was a rogue wind—like what happens with the waves."

His beautiful white teeth showed in a grin, which was partly hidden by his untrimmed beard. She wondered if he'd resent her offering to trim it for him.

"Talking about waves, may I suggest a quick swim

before you tackle the dishes? I wouldn't be surprised if it rains this afternoon, and I want to get in some painting time."

Robyn joined him readily. It was already becoming quite warm, and while what she longed for was a bath after last night's lovemaking, she accepted the substitute without her earlier resentment.

"Do you have time to give me a swimming lesson?" she asked daringly as they waded hand in hand into the water.

"If you want," he agreed. "We'll start with how to control your breathing."

After ten minutes of practice, she assured him she understood the principle and he instructed her in how to synchronize her arm and leg movements. "Now float on your stomach and I'll support you by your waist," he informed her.

She followed directions and was quite proud of her progress. However, she lost all synchronization when she became aware of his hand sliding over her buttocks to trail between her legs. "Philip!" she sputtered, floundering to her feet. She was pulled tight against his chest, his arms an iron band binding her to him in a spasm of need.

She arched against him in an uncontrollable response, her mouth raised for his kiss. How many decades, eons, was it since he'd last kissed her?

His chest expanded in a huge sigh before he released her, his hands going to her shoulders to hold her away as she tried to keep contact. "No, you Lorelei," he growled, his voice firming as he gained control. "I don't know what it is about you, but neither one of us will be satisfied with one kiss, and we both know where that will lead us."

"Is that so bad?" she taunted him lightly, her fingers moving teasingly over the pelt across his chest. Surely he wasn't going to deny them, not after her body had felt the extent of his arousal! But there was nothing wrong with his will power, she found out ruefully, as he turned her around and, with a tap to her derriere, kept her in front of him while marching her out of the lagoon.

"The sky might look innocent, but I smell rain," he stated firmly, "and I have a painting that's only half-finished."

And nothing must interfere with that, Robyn agreed, however reluctantly. She scooped up their discarded clothes and shook out the sand before handing him his sulu. She found her body was already drying when she slipped her camisole over her head. Where before the salty residue had repelled her, she now savored the astringent quality that Philip had mentioned. If it rained, would Philip join her with a cake of soap to rinse it away? Her usually carefully groomed hair must look like a rat's nest, she thought with a grimace.

After doing the dishes, Robyn wandered down the beach and sat in the shade offered by a clump of palm trees and watched in silent fascination as Philip laid broad strokes of color across the large canvas. She'd never before observed the creation of a painting. Her job was to search out the finished product.

She found herself playing a game, trying to second-guess him as to which color on the palette he'd utilize next. But when a streak of cherry red was accented by a thin line of vermilion, followed by a bright orange, she gave up and decided to simply enjoy the result of his expertise. She was just thankful that he was once again able to recapture the mood that she'd shattered the morning before.

She didn't know if Philip had been aware of her joining him; he'd made no acknowledgment. Baylor, however, had opened one eye and thumped his tail twice in greeting before the lid drooped closed again. A lethargic feeling was now creeping over her and her lids seemed to develop weights, making it difficult to stay awake. The air was heavy with a mixture of salt from the ocean and earthy odors from the forest rising behind her. It was a new perfume—one that Robyn found surprisingly satisfying.

Baylor shifted his position closer to her and she scratched him tentatively behind the ear. Her past had been singularly free of animals, and she'd never willingly made contact with them, but the dog had acted as her protector when she'd been in the water and somehow he seemed to fit a different category. Slowly she drifted off.

She awoke with a start as Baylor rose from under her hand. He faced the house, his tail wagging, and Robyn turned to see what had caught his attention.

Serina stood in the doorway, shading her eyes as she stared at them across the stretch of sand. Even at this distance, Robyn saw she was as lovely as she remembered. The brightly colored dress tied over her firm breasts hung in loose folds to her ankles, accenting the proud carriage inherent in her race.

Robyn glanced at Philip to find his concentration still on his canvas, and she rose quickly to go to the girl, unable to understand the return of her resentment.

When Philip had said nothing about the less-than-adequate outfit she was wearing, she accepted that he probably couldn't see it well and she had pushed her lingering discomfort aside. But now she had to force herself to appear unconcerned about her minimal covering. Why hadn't she had the sense at least to check if her other costume had been dry? She'd known that the girl was coming.

Robyn knew that she looked sexy in the camisole and minuscule panties, and, illogical as it was, she admitted to being ruffled when Philip hadn't made the expected comment.

Her steps faltered a second as she chastised herself. She'd never played the temptress before! What was happening to her? Ever since coming here she'd felt the layers of constraint peeling away, and she admitted to being at a loss as to how to cope with the new person that was being exposed.

Drawing on her cloak of cool reserve, which had carried her through many trying situations, she approached the young woman. "Serina, I believe?" she asked. "Philip mentioned you might be coming today with fresh bread." She hid the wry grimace. Did that sound as possessive to the girl as it did to her? How Philip would laugh!

Serina's mouth lifted in a tentative smile that tested the possibility of friendship. She motioned to the loaf of bread on the table. "I didn't want to intrude yesterday." Her brown eyes were shy and guileless, and Robyn felt unexpectedly ashamed of her proprietary greeting. She was acting like the mistress of the house talking down to a tradesperson!

Robyn walked past Serina and into the hut, frowning with irritation. Why was she harboring this antagonistic feeling toward the girl? Still, even on that first day, she'd sensed Serina's resentment over her arrival. The frown deepened and she bit her lip. A disturbing vision flashed before her of the young, slender girl in Philip's arms as he lowered her to the bed.

How absolutely silly, Robyn reprimanded herself. She was too intelligent to allow so demeaning a feeling as jealousy to intrude. What Philip's conduct had been before she'd arrived—or would be after she left—was no concern of hers. They were both free agents who happened to be thrown together under what was fondly touted as "romantic conditions," and they had reacted in a predictable fashion.

"Do you want me to clean like I used to?" Serina asked eagerly. "You shouldn't spoil your vacation by working."

Something in her voice made Robyn turn, and she caught the hopeful look on Serina's face. Of course! Why hadn't she realized the answer? She'd never been this dense before! Philip had explained how the women searched for work to augment their husbands' incomes.

"You need what Philip pays you, don't you?" It was a statement rather than a question.

Serina nodded, her expression now anxious. "The last time he was able to come, my husband said that if

I save everything I make from working here, maybe then we'd have enough to afford a small place so we can be together when the baby is born."

Robyn's gaze dropped, and for the first time she noticed the bulge at Serina's waist. No wonder her gown was so free flowing instead of the snug fit that was more commonly worn. "When is it due?" she asked, feeling unaccountably guilty for her uncharitable thoughts.

Teeth flashed white against dusky skin as Serina beamed proudly. "In five months."

"Where does your husband work?" How he must miss having this lovely girl by his side!

"At a hotel they're building in Taveuni," she replied wistfully.

Mentally reviewing the map she'd studied before coming, Robyn finally placed the remote island on the far side of Vanua Levu. Robyn could imagine the difficulties facing Serina's husband when trying to make connections for a visit. Hadn't she discovered that herself?

"This work isn't too much for you?" She knew so little about pregnancies except that there seemed to be a lot of discomfort involved.

"Oh, no!" Serina protested gently. She placed the loaf in the metal bread box to protect it from the humidity and then crossed the room to roll up the thick mattress pad. "I air the bed each time I come so it doesn't develop mildew. At home I do it every day," she informed Robyn. She then told of the mosses that were dried to stuff the mattress. It explained the crackling sound the bed made.

Robyn hurried to assist her. Recalling the night's ending with love-dampened bodies, she realized this would be her daily chore. Looking at the evidence of tossed sheets on the bed, Robyn was surprised by the flush heating her cheeks. There was only one bed in the place. Where else would she be sleeping? And what was she acting so uptight about anyway? Certainly Serina's unconcern showed she viewed their sleeping together as normal.

Robyn helped spread the mattress over the back railing as she floundered over her reaction. What had happened between Philip and her was too new— there'd been no time to come to terms with the explosive awakening he'd triggered within her. She wasn't ready for the world to intrude on what was still too tender, too remarkable for a possibly careless inspection of what was an intensely private happening.

"What else has to be done?" Robyn asked, when Serina tackled the cleaning of the two-burner stove after refilling the kerosene reservoir.

"If you'd like to, check that the cans are in the right place. One sometimes gets pushed into the wrong group and Philip ends up with peas for dessert." The girl glanced over her shoulder, her smile gentle, showing the identical compassion that had invaded Robyn. "When he first arrived, he came up with the idea of placing notches in the shelves. He uses them as guides when it's dark so he doesn't make too many mistakes."

Her soft brown eyes grew sad as she met Robyn's gaze. "I'm glad you've come. He has suffered through much unhappiness. No man should face what he has to by himself." Her face flushed at her assumption and she bent over the stove to give it a final brisk polish.

"Has his sight failed noticeably since he came?" These were questions Robyn had an urgent need to have answered, questions she could never ask Philip, and she waited intently for Serina's response.

The girl frowned in thought for a moment. "When he first came, the only thing we noticed was that even with several candles lit, he could see little at night. But Pappa Nia mentioned the other day that he was worried. Philip came to visit in the afternoon and a heavy cloud cover developed while he was there. When it came time to leave, Pappa realized that Philip couldn't locate the path. Pappa made believe that he wanted to talk with him away from the babble of us women, but it was an excuse to show him the way back without letting him know that we were aware that his sight was getting worse."

Tears glistened in the girl's eyes, and Robyn closed hers to ease their burning as she recalled how now, even with the sun shining brightly, he had to rely on Baylor to lead him to the shore. Was his vision failing that rapidly? Oh, Philip! Her hand pressed against her breast to ease the uncomfortable tightening triggered by the thought.

"He doesn't light candles anymore," Robyn murmured, reaching for the wooden holder that he'd used the night before. Her fingers moved abstractedly over the carvings until the art connoisseur in her caused her attention to focus on the article.

"This is beautiful," she said with admiration as she examined the birds in flight done in bas-relief. "Was this made locally?" It hadn't been stained or sanded to bring out the best of the wood grain, but the soaring lines of the birds—were they pelicans?—were done lovingly. She had a friend who was always searching for something like this for her gift shop.

Serina looked at her with surprise. "Why, Philip made it. When Pappa Nia finds some wood that looks like it would do for carving, he brings it to Philip. He works on it at night or during the rainy season when he can't paint."

The candlestick was replaced carefully on the table. Oh, Philip! the voice cried deep within her. To have such a need to constantly express oneself artistically! How could life be so cruel as to gift a man with such creativity, only to torture him by dimming his sight.

What hell he must have gone through when he'd first found out. She could now understand his need to escape to this island by himself to come to terms with the cruel trick fate had dealt him. That he'd been able to adjust by changing his painting technique gave an indication of his versatility and the indomitable strength of his character. And she'd had the audacity to intrude with the intention of poking holes in his hard-won peace of mind.

She'd been with him but a short time, but she was certain that he had no desire to return to the public adulation that had been his and, she suspected, no need for the money his new paintings would undoubtedly command. He would return to the world he'd rejected only when he was ready to, and only on his own terms.

"Would you like to see where I get the drinking water from?" Serina asked, breaking into her thoughts. "I always bring him a bucketful since I don't think he can see the path too well through the woods." Serina took the bucket and headed into the forest rising behind the bure.

Robyn looked askance at the narrow path and the looming trees that seemed to reach out hungrily at the gliding figure disappearing into their depths. Gathering a firm hold on her courage, Robyn plunged in after Serina. Usually she assiduously avoided even the manicured park across from her apartment, but in the past two days she'd done many things she'd never before considered possible. Clenching her hands, she plunged into this new unknown. One more breakaway could hardly make any difference!

First the odor assailed her, then the sounds—or rather the lack of them. The warm air was humid, and redolent with the surprisingly pleasant pungent aroma of gently decaying vegetation. The thick brush acted as an insulation against the sound of the waves. It wasn't until then that she was aware of how that ceaseless rhythm had become a soothing background. Now there was a different rhythm caused by the breeze sighing through the upper reaches of the trees.

Serina was waiting for her around the bend and Robyn breathed a sigh of relief. While her intelligence had registered that she was perfectly safe, some long-buried primitive part of her still quailed in apprehension over the unknown.

"Pappa Nia put up this vine so Philip could follow it should he ever need to go for more water," Serina informed her.

Her hand rested on a braided line that was tied waist

high along the side of the path, and Robyn marveled at the thoughtfulness of the people who watched over Philip with such unobtrusive care. But she'd noticed the pride with which they carried themselves, and it followed that they'd be sensitive to it in another.

They traveled another hundred feet until they were stopped by a cliff rising a good hundred feet above them. From its edge a tiny stream of water cascaded into a small pool no larger than a bathtub.

"This was only a muddy hole, but Pappa Nia dug it out and lined it with stones so the water stays clean," Serina said, dipping the bucket into the clear pool.

"I can't wait to take a bath!" Robyn exclaimed, thinking longingly of the scented soap and shampoo left behind in the hotel. Why had Philip intimated there was no place to bathe? she wondered with some annoyance.

"Oh, no!" Serina objected. "This is only for drinking. The stream runs only after we have rain. In the dry season this all dries up and we have to bring the water from the other side of the island. You could, however," she conceded, softening on seeing Robyn's disappointment, "pour a bucket over yourself when you see it full like it is now."

Robyn shuddered at the primitive picture evoked by Serina's concession, yet she had no doubt that she'd be reduced to doing just that.

Dark clouds lined the horizon when they returned. How had Philip been able to predict rain? she wondered. After Serina left, she again joined Philip. The canvas was almost done, and she was caught once more by the sweeping sense of happiness it depicted.

"It's good," she murmured in appreciation.

He turned from his close scrutiny to look toward her. "In what way?"

It was a professional question. She knew he was not seeking compliments but asking for an evaluation, and she paused to sort out her reactions. After all, wasn't this what she was trained to do?

"I've seen only two of your paintings, but in both you've used virtually the same palette yet managed to create an entirely different mood. In this one, I feel a spiraling joy, a released happiness." She paused, recalling her strong reaction on first seeing the one Winslow had brought back.

He nodded his head in appreciation. "I wondered if I could put it across." He cocked his head then, the devilish smile she'd learned to appreciate tugging on his lips. "And what was your reaction to the one I sent off with your boss?"

Robyn had herself under control and sidestepped the intent of his question. "You'd better be prepared. When Winslow hangs that one, you may well have a stream of women beating a path here," she returned dryly.

His smile deepened. "It brought you," he observed succinctly.

She glared at him. What did he mean by that? "Only on Winslow's insistence!" she snapped.

His dark brow arched and Robyn found herself forced to reevaluate her contention. Hadn't she, even while offering protestations to Winslow, been eager to be on her way to see what time had done to this man she'd met only once before? And, she conceded further, to see if that initial attraction still held the same power?

It did, she admitted. That had been the reason for her rapid and uncharacteristic capitulation, she now realized. No man had been able to climb over—no, completely demolish—the wall that had protected her secret self. She had suspected the deeply hidden passion, had been afraid of its effect on her once released. Yet Philip, with one kiss, had brought it into immediate bloom. She only hoped that when she left his island, the flower would fade rapidly from lack of nourishment. Once safely back in L.A., this aberration would be treated for what it was, a momentary lapse to be marked off as an experience and given a quiet burial.

She turned from his mocking expression to notice the increased bank of dark clouds. "It looks like the rain you forecast will be arriving soon," she said, glad for the change of subject.

He raised his head in a listening attitude and Robyn, doing the same, became aware of the unusual quiet. The birds had stopped their twittering and the crickets for once were silenced. Even the long palm fronds had stopped their ceaseless rustling.

The stillness became threatening, and Robyn stepped closer to Philip in an unconscious need for his reassurance. Apprehension sent a prickling sensation down her spine and her eyes widened on seeing the ocean. Minutes before it had been unruffled, vibrant blue; now it had turned into a sullen gray. Far out she could see the building, whitecapped waves.

"We'd better get a move on," Philip ordered hurriedly, sliding his painting supplies into his carrying case. "That front feels like it'll be on us soon."

"I'll carry the canvas," she offered, and she lifted it carefully, permitting Philip to snap the easel closed.

"Thanks. Just be careful, it's still wet," he warned unnecessarily as Baylor positioned himself against his leg and the two led the way back to the bure.

The first gust of wind hit her just as they reached the hut and almost succeeded in tearing the canvas from her hands. She braced it against the table and hurried to rescue the bedding still airing on the back railing while Philip went around lowering the rolled matting over the openings and fastening them down.

Robyn lit a candle against the increasing darkness as Philip lowered the last protective mat. The palm trees were making up for their moment of rest; the long fronds were whipping in a clattering, atonal frenzy.

The rain was announced with a flash of lightning that lit the darkened interior. The crash of thunder came right on its heels. The rain descended then in a roar that the roof's thatching was unable to muffle.

Robyn found herself moving closer to the seemingly unconcerned man. Before, she had been able to ignore thunderstorms, protected within walls of glass and concrete. Now, with the matting looking appallingly fragile, she felt uncomfortably vulnerable.

When a particularly vicious gust tore at the building, she couldn't stop her cry of fright or her leap into his arms. They closed around her as she buried her face into the curve of his neck.

"It'll pass soon," he reassured her soothingly. "It always does."

But soon wasn't quick enough. She groaned as she pushed her face into closer contact with his warm skin when another clash of thunder rolled menacingly overhead. As a child she'd been frightened of loud storms, but she had thought her fear had been successfully buried. Was nothing safe? she wailed inwardly. Did every emotion have to be bared before this man?

She shivered, and she realized it was as much from the lowered temperature ushered in by the storm's cold front as it was from her inner distress.

He drew her closer. "You're cold. The temperature drops like this frequently, but it usually warms up again after the storm passes," he said consolingly, his hand moving comfortingly along the curve of her back.

Robyn was unaware of when things had changed. One minute he was the solicitous protector, the next he was a desiring male. The soothing pass of his hands changed from a calming glide to a passionate kneading, as if he were intent on relearning the texture of her skin.

"There's one place we can go where I can warm you," he growled huskily into her hair. "Remember?"

Robyn nodded, helpless before the surging need he so easily triggered, and lifted her face for his kiss that would start the process.

His mouth fitted over hers in a perfect match until he was sated with that initial meeting. His lips then moved with a roving thoroughness that became a sensuous promise of the delights ahead.

Robyn marveled at his expertise even as her legs

lost their ability to support her, causing her to lean against him. Immediately on contact, her body softened and flowed, melting to mold in perfect conformation with his hard thrusting body. They moved as one to the waiting bed, the chilling drop in the temperature forgotten.

8

When Robyn awoke all sounds of the storm were gone. The light filtering into the room indicated there were still several hours of daylight left.

She gave a contented sigh and snuggled closer into the warm cocoon created by Philip's body curved at her back. Tentacles of the dream that wasn't a dream clung—tender molding hands, a moist searching mouth, and finally, a hard muscular body demanding as much as it gave.

Philip shifted slightly in his sleep to better accommodate her form. His hand moved up her rib cage, searching for and finally finding its resting place when it cupped the soft fullness of her breast. A small tremor ran through her at the contact. What was it about this man that had her responding this way?

The sensations produced by her naked back pressing against him, by his arm holding her close, and the way his breath became a warm caress as it whispered across her cheek mesmerized her. A smile of utter contentment curved her lips as she marveled over the lassitude which enfolded her.

It was Philip who had brought her to this blissful state—this man whose kisses could melt while they seared, whose hands could excite as they soothed, whose body could take as it gave the ultimate of passion.

Hearing their movements, Baylor rose and stretched, giving a prodigious yawn. He then padded over to the bed to look hopefully at the occupants, his tail swinging in a lazy arc.

Robyn surprised herself by patting the dog's head, but she couldn't stop her startled reaction when his rough tongue reached out in a damp slurp.

The broad chest pressed against her back moved in a silent laugh. "She tastes good, doesn't she, old chap?" Philip quipped as he leaned across her to gently tug the animal's ear. He then demonstrated his own approval by running flipping licks along her bared shoulder.

"Enough!" she squealed as she laughingly evaded his foray. "I admit to needing a bath, but—"

She was pulled back, to be anchored by Philip's muscular thigh. He cupped her face and glared menacingly at her. "And where do you think you're going, my proud beauty? I have a need to perform lascivious things upon your person."

She saw the laughter dancing in his eyes and couldn't help responding in kind. "Oh, prithee, sir, unhand me. I am a poor castaway on your island and beg for your protection and benevolence."

"Benevolence, shmevolence, call it what you wish, my sweet wench. I intend to lavish it on you," he growled, his devilish smile very much in evidence. His mouth found hers, effectively halting their teasing exchange.

"You have to do something about that mustache," she informed him as he kissed an erotic trail down the curve of her throat.

"Does it bother you?" he asked, moving up to her ear to explore the territory.

"Well, it does get in the way," she murmured, trying not to act distracted as she arched her neck.

He raised his head and shifted to one elbow as he brushed the offending mustache. "Serina gives me an occasional trim, and I guess I could stand one again."

Robyn was beginning to like the native girl, but the intrusion of her name at this time cooled her affection. Philip had shifted enough so that with an added shove from her, she was able to send him off-balance and permit her escape before he could stop her.

"There's no better time than now," she said from the safety of the middle of the room.

"Later, love. Surely we have better things to do first?" he wheedled.

"You wouldn't say that if you could feel what's happening to the skin on my face," she accused him.

"You win—this time," he concurred with an exaggerated sigh of resignation. He sat up and swung his long legs out of the bed. "Lead on. Where is the shearing to take place?"

"Shearing is right," Robyn agreed. Taking a critical look at his heavy crop of hair, she was having second thoughts. What had she let herself in for? She'd never cut hair before! But anything was better than the shaggy mane he now sported, she reassured herself bracingly. And the mustache certainly got in the way of their kisses.

"Since I'm the one who will have to clean up, I suggest we do it outside," she said firmly. No use having him suspect the qualms she was experiencing!

Her lips quirked as he dragged his feet like a little boy being led reluctantly to a barber. He unfastened the door, letting in the sunshine, and sat down resignedly on the wash bench. This ability to relax and tease was a new part of him that she found most endearing.

"I do need scissors," she informed him.

"They're in the drawer," he sighed.

"Drawer?" she asked, looking around the spartan room. "What drawer?"

"In the cabinet by the stove, the only drawer there is," he returned patiently.

She decided not to dignify that with an answer. "Where's the comb?" she questioned after retrieving the scissors.

"What's this, a production number?" he asked suspiciously. "Mine disintegrated a while back, so I don't have one."

"It looks like it," she returned smartly, digging hers out of her pocketbook. "Now sit still while I give you a once-over-lightly."

"Do I get a lollipop afterward? I'd like a red one, sweet as your lips." He leered with exaggerated relish.

"What do you think this is, a massage parlor?" she answered haughtily.

"An admirable idea," he returned, his hands mov-

ing testingly along her thighs as she made a first
tentative cut.

"You are living dangerously," she said sternly,
denying the quiver his touch incited. "You forget that I
have scissors in my hands."

"My turn will come," he muttered darkly.

"Are you trying to intimidate me, sir? I shall have to
report you to the barbers' union!"

When had she felt so happy? she wondered with a
mounting delight as she bent to her task. Of course,
their exchange was less than intelligent, but she
couldn't deny the resulting bubbling lightheartedness
invading her.

Keeping a mental picture before her of the way
Philip had looked when she'd first seen him two years
ago, first she snipped and trimmed his mustache and
beard before starting on his shoulder-length hair.
Philip's expression gradually changed from apprehension to one of resignation.

"I hope you know what you're doing," he grunted
when the scissors grazed his ear.

"I hope so, too, since this is the first haircut I've
attempted."

"Now she tells me I'm a blasted guinea pig!" he
groaned. "Well, you're the one who has to look at me.
I hope you'll be filled with proper remorse."

She pursued a straggling end and lopped it off with
a sense of accomplishment. "It's not bad," she reassured him as she stepped back to check her tonsorial
expertise. "The sides balance nicely and there are
only a few thin spots that will grow out in time."

"Thanks heaps," he muttered as he fingered the
finished result. "I have complete sympathy for Sam-

son. I can imagine how he must have felt after waking up to find himself shorn."

"You mean you'll now have an excuse for the loss of all your strength?" she mocked.

"I'll show you what I've lost," he warned. He was off the bench before she could move. His arms curled around her, pulling her snug against his chest. The sun was bright on them, and he examined her face with a moment of fierce intensity before his expression relaxed under his teasing smile. "Science could well benefit from our research into this matter," he mused with an academic pomposity. "Is a kiss more stimulating before or after a haircut? I don't believe I've read anything about it, and I don't think Samson recorded his findings on the matter!"

"Silly!" Robyn laughed before his mouth found and covered hers. She soon discovered she was a poor subject to participate in a scientific research project. She was unable to keep the necessary unbiased objectivity.

Her mouth moved under his, seeking while he found. Her tongue parted his lips, invading while his conquered. Her hands touched and caressed while his possessed.

"Well, what do you think?" he asked thickly when he finally raised his head.

Robyn blinked her eyes dazedly, wondering at first what he was referring to. "I think," she said with a breathless laugh, "that this requires a little more investigating before you have all the necessary scientific data."

"My thoughts exactly," he agreed solemnly. Then,

with a whoop of joyous laughter, he swept her up in his arms and carried her inside to stand her by the bed.

"You know what?" she said pertly to hide the quiver of anticipation when Philip found the bow holding her chemise top. "What you should really research is the strange reaction one has when on these tropical islands. Since I've been here, I can't seem to keep my clothes on!"

"That's because you still have a hang-up about wearing them!" he teased. His fingers hooked in her bikini pants, and as he pulled them down, moist kisses were planted across the smooth skin of her abdomen.

His sulu was abandoned and she quivered under the twin assault of his seeking hands and the visual picture of his bronzed body. "Just because you're a sun worshiper . . ." she began before he tipped her onto the bed.

"I'll show you what I worship," he said huskily, covering her with his body. "I intend to pay homage to every square inch of your delectable silken-soft flesh, to say incantations over you until you're helplessly bound to my will."

And he proved the extent of his predicted ability with every touch, with every kiss, with every murmured growl that was a seductive language in itself.

The next morning, Philip left with his canvas and paints after an early breakfast. Conscious of a deep inner contentment, Robyn hummed softly as she followed the regime suggested by Serina. The bedding was aired over the back railing, but she cheated a little by washing the dishes with the fresh water remaining in the bucket. With the heavy rain they'd had the day before, she was certain the pool would be full.

She swallowed her initial hesitation before stepping into the verdant forest, pail in hand. If her prediction was true, she intended to have that promised sluicing, even without the benefit of soap. Her hair was salt laden and completely unmanageable. The small stream draining the pool would have to suffice as a place to do the necessary rinsing of her clothes.

The day before, she'd followed Serina down the path, blind to the mysterious forest that seemed to press all around her. But now her trained eye was intrigued by the varied foliage, the play of shadows where the sun sent misty beams of light through every available opening. How was it that she'd never appreciated the nuances of colors displayed so abundantly in their natural environment? What had it been in her past that had caused her to be so blind that she could only see nature's beauty after it had been transposed onto canvas?

She chewed her lip as she followed the question to its startling conclusion. She'd chosen a vocation that permitted her to concentrate on the beautiful things in life. She'd molded a lifestyle that gave her the control to eliminate that which was ugly or unpredictable. Her apartment reflected that obsession. Anything that jarred was ruthlessly eliminated, even though in itself it might appeal to her.

Ghosts from her childhood pulled at her now: a mother who was obsessed with maintaining an immaculate house, whose constant berating made a sensitive child become afraid of going outside to play lest she track any clinging dirt into the house; a child who soon found that the only way to gain approval was to maintain a spotless appearance. She recalled how when she'd inadvertently spill something, her heart would race in panic as she waited for her mother's strident scold. Was this why she never walked in the park, and refused invitations to barbecues from friends who lived in the country? she mused in wonder.

The small glen opened before her and she pushed her disturbing thoughts from her mind. The rain had given the waterfall more force and it splashed musically into the pool. There was no need to feel guilty about her planned rinsing off.

She almost dropped the bucket when she poured the first pailful over her head. She'd assumed that it would be as warm as the ocean, and the shock of the colder water left her gasping. However, it was truly refreshing and she continued her sluicing, though more carefully.

Returning, she hung her rinsed camisole and bikini underwear over the railing and draped the two gaily flowered sulus around her. If she alternated the procedure each day, she would at least have clean clothes to wear.

When she'd finished, she went to the front opening and looked down the beach to see that Philip was immersed in his painting. Her gaze drifted back to the interior of the building and moved to the corner section that was draped with woven mats. Winslow had said he'd seen a number of finished canvases, and that was the only possible place for them to be.

Philip, she knew, would be painting for a few more

hours. Quelling her feeling of guilt, she moved pur-
posefully to the corner and rolled back the mat. After
all, she reminded herself bracingly, this was the reason
for her coming—to try and convince Philip to have
Winslow act as his agent. Besides, the paintings would
certainly mildew and deteriorate if left in this humid
climate, and that loss to the world could not be
considered.

There were two dozen canvases, and she carried
them outside to prop them against the wall so she
could view them in the light. Two, she realized, were
heartbreaking attempts at painting Serina and Pappa
Nia. One had a harsh slash of black paint across it,
giving an indication of the deep frustration Philip had
experienced when he'd realized he could no longer
see well enough to mix the fine nuances of color
needed to bring the skin tones to life. How had he
managed to survive that dreadful period? she agonized.

She examined the rest, seeing the evolution of his
new style. The first few showed an angry need to
express his frustration. They were undisciplined slashes of dark pigment, undoubtedly expressive of his
inner rage, and she swallowed hard against the responsive tightening in her throat, feeling the pain as if
it had been hers.

She wondered at what point in the past two years
he had come to realize that those bold strokes held a
magic of their own. Some canvases must have been
destroyed, because the rest showed his newfound
talent in full bloom. Yes, there were angry ones, but
the paint was now applied with an artist's sure hand.
She moved on to the more serene ones, showing the

mending of his soul. They reminded her of the peaceful lagoon, and it seemed as if it would require no effort to dive into the luminous colors and explore the reef hidden in their depths.

When had he finally come to life again enough to feel the sharpened emotions conveyed in the last two paintings? The one Winslow had brought back had been expressive of a man's passionate need, and she shivered slightly on recalling how intensely she had responded to it.

She examined the last one before her with growing appreciation. The paint had still not hardened completely, indicating that it must have been the one produced after Winslow had left. It reminded her of the sea gulls in flight. Like the birds, it depicted the soaring freedom of emotions reaching beyond man's limitation. What a gift was given to this man that he could take emotions that many couldn't even express in words and translate them into vibrant exclamations with the use of pigments!

And his latest . . . She glanced over her shoulder to where Philip was applying a contrasting curl of yellow ocher against a bright yellow. He had started that painting the day after she arrived. A spiral of exquisite joy threaded through her. Had that time spent in each other's arms been the inspiration for the happiness expressed on his canvas? She hugged herself with the sheer delight of the idea.

After the paintings were returned, she sat at the table, her smooth brow furrowed in thought. Her flights of fancy, delightful though they might be, were back under control. She had a job to perform. What would be the best way to approach Philip about letting her take the canvases back with her? She was certain that his angry denunciation on the beach had been in retaliation for her demeaning accusations. He couldn't still be harboring that terrible idea that she was here trading her body for the rights to his paintings.

Robyn shifted restlessly on the chair as the niggling doubt intruded. Surely Philip had felt some of the wonder that she'd experienced. Dear Lord, was she living in a fool's paradise by assuming that he felt as she did?

The balloon that she'd been floating on punctured, tumbling her back to reality. Feeling disoriented, as if she'd fallen into a time warp, she stared around the hut with a dazed expression. What was she doing here, dressed indecently in two inadequate pieces of cloth? What had possessed her to give herself so wantonly to a virtual stranger?

Her first overwhelming urge was to put on her suit, as if once properly dressed, she could retreat behind a shield and deny all that had transpired the past three days. She was half out of her chair before sagging back. What then? reason asked. No matter what she wore or did, the fact remained that she was trapped here for the remainder of the two weeks.

She had no idea how long she sat in dejected thought as unrelated images squirreled around in her mind. The room finally closed in on her and she left its shelter in a rush, giving in to the need to walk off the strange sensations invading her. There was a feeling of crisis, as if this day, this hour, she had to reach some decision and that it could well trigger a turning point in her life.

There were only two directions she could take along the beach. One led back to where Serina lived, or she could go the other way, which was unexplored. But Philip was painting there. She had no desire to go to the village, so she turned resolutely in the other direction.

Philip was facing the lagoon, and while she didn't know the extent of his ability to see, she suspected safety lay in hugging the forest edge.

She held her breath when Baylor raised his head, but he only gave a few red-tongued pants before settling back to sleep. Philip, she saw, continued squeezing some paint on his palette. The sand was an effective muffle to her passage in spite of his acute hearing.

She walked until the sharp pricking on her feet warned her that the character of the shoreline had changed. She'd gone beyond the small lagoon and found this new area had only a thin covering of sand over the coral outcroppings.

She picked her way carefully to a large plank washed high on the beach by some long-forgotten storm. She sat gingerly on a weathered section and contemplated the scene spread before her.

About a hundred yards out, the breaking waves made a white fringe, marking the protective reef that surrounded the island. From this angle, the wind blew uninhibitedly from across the Pacific, giving more force to the waves rolling onto the beach. She could see that in comparison the small lagoon where Philip had built his bure was special, a little slice of Eden. Was she the Eve to his Adam? Yet, what right had she to introduce the fateful apple, tempting him away from the peace and security he'd created after untold pain and tears?

Torn by the conflicting emotions, she sat with arms crossed tight over her abdomen, as if the pressure could still the unease her disturbing questions had aroused. Never before had she been torn with such indecision as to where her duty lay. If she brought Philip's paintings back with her, she knew her longed-for partnership in the Cornell Gallery was assured. And Philip the artist would be on display.

But what of Philip Holt the man? A deep sigh tore from her. She could only suspect the tears and rage that had had to be expended before Philip had been able to come to terms with the blow that he'd been dealt. This place was his refuge, but what would it become if the world knew where he had disappeared to? And knowing the avid nature of tourists, she could guess at what would happen. She closed her eyes against the vision of them descending en masse, destroying the peace he'd struggled to create. How could she in all conscience be instrumental in destroying what he'd built?

If Philip had wanted that exposure he'd have consented to Winslow's inducements. Instead he'd refused his handsome offer, sending him away with the painting as a consolation.

She frowned as she thought about that painting. Why had Philip done that? Surely he must have known that any art dealer of Winston's caliber would take that as a challenge to possess more?

It brought you here, didn't it? The forgotten words

whispered in her ear, bringing a new meaning. He had shown that he'd remembered the color of her dress she'd worn at that long-ago meeting. Had he been told at the time the name of the gallery she'd worked for? Had he used the picture as a deliberate lure? What had he hinted to Winslow that had made her employer so adamant about her coming here?

Unexpected prickles of pleasure danced along her nerve endings, but she immediately suppressed them. If Philip had been that interested in her, he'd surely have made the effort to locate her. There had been that electrical meeting of eyes across the room, which had resulted in the awareness that had remained with her over the ensuing months. She would have offered no objection to knowing him better. Instead he'd become engaged.

But that engagement was no longer valid. She chewed the soft lining of her lip as she tried to make sense of her scattered thoughts.

There were so many questions that needed answers. Meanwhile she had ten days to get through. Ten days with an exciting and virile man. Who was she, to fight what she had no control over? She could accept it, calling it destiny, kismet, but she knew it was the undeniable attraction of the man that made her decision so easy.

All ambiguity faded before her acceptance. Already her pulse beat with a new life as she rose and turned her steps back the way she'd come. When she returned to L.A. there would be time enough to tuck these two weeks away as a momentary lapse.

Meanwhile, she couldn't deny the chemistry that drew her back to the bure and the man who could so easily send her senses reeling. For the remaining time she would forget all else and revel in being the woman he'd created, the woman that she never knew had been hidden deep within her.

9

When she reached where Philip was painting, she sank in the sand next to Baylor. The dog stretched out beside her, offering his stomach to be rubbed. She obliged him bemused by the totally new Robyn that was emerging. Previously, she had assiduously avoided animals in any form, but this faithful dog was showing her what she'd missed.

Philip glanced over his shoulder at her, a smile of greeting on his lips. "Come to admire the artist?" he teased.

She couldn't deny the flash of pleasure she felt at the warmth in his look. "More likely his painting," she returned dryly. "Is it almost finished?"

"This one corner needs strengthening," he admitted, returning his concentration to his work.

Though they didn't speak, she was aware of the comfortable relaxed feeling flowing between them. He stood with his long muscular legs spread apart, his toes digging in the sand as a brace as he examined his creation.

The palm fronds waving overhead permitted intermittent splashes of sunlight to gild his teak-colored body and touch the silver glints in his dark hair. He was a man in his prime, and her heart beat with a heavy thud as her blood seemed to thicken in her veins. She fought the urge to go to him, to wrap her arms around him and adjust her soft curves to the strong lines of his back.

Would he put down his palette and take her in his arms, sink with her into the sand as they had done once before? She became vibrantly aware of the way her breasts strained against the restrictive material.

Philip selected a tube of paint from the careful alignment in his box and raised it close to his eyes to peer at it to make certain it was the right choice. Her heart made a painful flip at the evidence of his affliction. *Oh, my darling . . . my darling,* she murmured silently in deep compassion, and pressed her hand tightly over her lips before the betraying sound escaped.

Memories intruded of his intent expression when he examined her face from inches away. Was that the only way he could make out her features? What must it be like to see everything in an indistinct haze unless illuminated by a high-intensity light? What could be more cruel to an artist than to have his world disintegrate into an ill-defined blur?

She sat with hands clenched as she deliberately made her eyes lose their focus. Philip became a shadowed form outlined by the blue lagoon, which had lost its beautiful color variations. The beach was an off-white blur, all character disappearing when the shells, the occasional pieces of driftwood and the seaweed lost their identity.

Oh, Philip . . . oh, my darling! The words whispered in her heart as swelling tears dimmed everything further. This was how he was forced to view the world.

That evening, when they ate a dinner made late by their reluctance to end their swim in the lagoon, Robyn furthered her indoctrination. She didn't explain her strange need to share Philip's handicap, but she didn't light the candle after the sun made its rapid plunge into the sea.

She soon saw the necessity of keeping the coffee mug in its correct place and, after barking her shin on the chair, of replacing the furniture in the same position. Such little but vital things! she mused, and realized the spartan look to the room had its reason.

When they went to bed that night, her new awareness made her respond to Philip with a new passion. He had suffered alone too long. Her compassion had her longing to absorb some of the hurt, to show him that as long as she was with him, she was willing to share his frustrations and perhaps ease them with that sharing.

Robyn never questioned why she was responding this way. When he gathered her close for their final union, she opened herself to him, becoming all things —mother, wife, mistress—in her overwhelming need to give of herself.

Later, when they lay entwined, their breathing finally returned to normal, he buried his face between her breasts and whispered hoarsely, "Oh, God,

Robyn, you're beautiful, so beautiful," and she was content that he had sensed something of what she had offered.

Serina arrived the next day with the loaf of bread and several eggs. "The young chickens are starting to lay, so we have extra. I thought you'd like some," she offered.

Under her arm was a wood figure, and she placed it carefully on the table. "You were interested in Philip's carving the other day, so I thought you'd like to see one," she said shyly. "He hasn't finished many, but I loved this one and he gave it to me for my birthday. Pappa Nia has several, and Philip made one of my head so my John could take it back with him and perhaps not forget me." Serina's expression was pensive when she referred to her absent husband.

"I doubt he could do that," Robyn returned, but her attention was focused on the foot-long carving. It was of Baylor sitting in a position she'd often seen him in, with his head cocked alertly to one side as he tried to anticipate his master's next move.

It was beautifully executed. How often had Philip's talented hands stroked his beloved dog, striving to retain the memory of his conformation so that he could reproduce it with such loving care? A shiver went through her on recalling those same sensitive fingers caressing every inch of her body. Did they retain this detailed a memory of her?

Robyn stroked the smooth wood, marveling over the varied talents of the man. Was this then to be the next step in his development? His talent could never remain bottled up. After seeing the way he'd adjusted his painting style, she knew the artist in him would always need an outlet to express itself. But oh, the pain he must go through when forced to make that transition!

"Has he ever tried a larger carving?" Robyn questioned.

"He's asked for bigger pieces of wood to work with, but driftwood frequently splits as it dries. Pappa cut down a tree and cut it into sections, but it hasn't dried enough yet to use. It has a fine grain and he hopes Philip will be happy with it."

On leaving, Serina paused by the back railing where the bedding was already airing and longingly fingered the lace-edged camisole still draped there. "Are these very expensive?" she asked wistfully. "I would love to buy one for when John comes next time."

Recalling the fancy price she'd paid for that bit of whimsy, Robyn knew it was far beyond what this girl could ever afford. "I'll trade it for one of your dresses you can't wear at present," she offered. "These sulus are made to wrap around a man's narrow hips, but I find the slightest breeze has me exposed to the elements," Robyn admitted with a rueful laugh.

Serina beamed with delight. "I'll go right now and bring one over this morning," she promised, and hurried off as if afraid Robyn might change her mind.

Now what made her do that? she mused, disconcerted over her uncharacteristic benevolence. Was this another facet of the intense giving that had been part of their lovemaking the night before? She pursued the thought no further; it was too complex and confusing. Last night had been a special experience, and it seemed that now that it had surfaced, the soft and sharing part of her refused to be submerged again.

She waited to take her bath until Serina returned, shyly offering two dresses in trade. "You'll need a change," she said, and left quickly with the camisole clasped to her breast, her eyes bright in anticipation of her husband's reaction on seeing it on her, her dusky skin glowing through the provocative inserts of lace.

The days passed in a golden haze that Robyn never questioned. She'd been blessed with a two-week hiatus from a way of life that was becoming increasingly more unreal. The curved beach became her world, and the tall, dominant man its king. When he drew her into his arms at night, she knew an indescribable bliss as they explored every nuance of passion with a fevered intensity. It was as if they knew they had to put a lifetime of emotion into the short time allotted to them.

A routine was established. After breakfast, Philip took his paint supplies a short distance down the beach to set up his canvas under the swaying palms while Robyn did the small amount of cleaning and went for a fresh bucket of water. After her quick sluicing, she'd rinse out the clothes they'd worn the day before. When the sun was at its zenith, she'd make tall glasses of tea, made pleasantly tart with a slice of carambola, the exotic yellow star-shaped fruit that Serina brought from a tree that grew in their compound. They didn't have the luxury of ice, but Robyn discovered it made little difference as they shared the short break. The person who had demanded perfection in her food didn't exist in this world.

Philip had been startled when she'd first taken the tea to him, but now the ritual was a pleasant break in the day that he seemed to appreciate. They would then take a quick swim before he returned to his easel.

Robyn looked forward to that pause. In Los Angeles, every minute at work had been crammed with details that kept her busy. Now, while she felt indecently contented with the unpressured hours, she needed this small time to talk and have human contact.

They shared humorous as well as somber incidents that had happened to them in that faraway world that, even while they were talking about it, seemed like it belonged to another lifetime. It was during one of those sessions that Robyn discovered the events around his engagement.

"It happened during a moment's madness," he admitted dryly. "My ego had me sitting on top of the world. I decided I'd tried pretty much everything; the only thing I hadn't tried was the husband-father bit. After careful consideration, I chose Maureen as having the most desirable qualities. She was lovely to look at and had all the social graces. Gad, what fools we mortals be!" His voice was tinged with bitterness as he paused to take a swallow of tea.

"Then gradually I realized something wasn't quite right. The proportions were all wrong when I mixed paint for a desired skin color. It wasn't until Max Cline, a close friend and my severest critic, visited me and asked what new technique I was exploring that I knew I had a problem."

He stared unseeingly for long minutes over the blue water, the lines bracketing his mouth deepening, telling of the horror of the discovery that he was reliving. Robyn sat on the sand beside him, aching to touch him, to share his pain, but she remained still, her clenched hands telling of her restraint.

He finally drew a deep breath and returned to the present. "The eye doctor put me immediately into the hospital and I had to endure a long series of tests. The diagnosis was progressive degeneration of the optic nerve, and more importantly, there was no treatment available. Though they couldn't predict when, the final outcome would be total blindness." He spat the words out as if they had an acid taste.

"I went into shock, which I guess was natural. How does an artist exist when he can no longer see? I was feeling like a martyr when I offered Maureen her freedom; I couldn't be bitter when she agreed with barely contained relief. One of the qualities I'd chosen her for was her love of the social life and her brilliance as a hostess. I suppose she had visions of being trapped in a dark house where the lights were never lit. After all, what use has a blind man for lights?" His brittle laugh caused Robyn to flinch.

"When the word got out, I was inundated with pity from well-meaning friends until I felt smothered. I didn't need it. I was wallowing in my own mammoth self-pity. I decided I had to get away from it all, to somehow find a way to come to grips with what was to be my future." He closed his eyes to hide the desolation. "The day you arrived I realized my sight had slipped another notch, that my time was running out."

He ground the base of the tea glass into the sand so it would sit upright. "And that, my dear Robyn, is the sad but true story of one Philip Holt," he said in a tightly constrained voice. "And why in the devil I've spilled it all out, I have no idea; but thanks for listening.''

Robyn was unaware she was moving until she found herself kneeling in the sand beside him and cradling his head against her breasts. *Philip, oh, my dearest darling,* she mouthed silently, her face buried in his thick hair. Her hand moved in soothing caresses over the bare shoulders, kneading with gentle fingers the taut muscles banding their length. She had evidently arrived in his hour of need, but there was no pain in the realization that he'd taken her that first morning in an effort to block out his alarm. Remembering his relaxed expression afterward, she was content that he'd succeeded.

He shifted so he could wrap his arms around her waist, and they stayed that way for a long time. Dear Lord, she thought, how could he have tolerated her that day when she'd heaped her accusations on him while he was struggling to come to grips with his awful discovery!

Robyn was unaware of the tears moistening her cheeks; her only conscious need was to help this man come to terms with the grief he'd kept buried.

Her heart seemed to swell with an all-encompassing love. She placed little kisses along his forehead, his temple, and when she reached down to his cheek, she found moisture there, telling of his tears. She cupped his face with aching tenderness and kissed away the evidence even as her tears further dampened his cheek. Had he ever been able to find the relief of tears before? she wondered.

His arms tightened around her and she found herself braced across his raised knees as he buried his face into the warm curve of her neck. She caressed him with gentle understanding as the silent sobs moved his chest. Time held no meaning, and she had no idea how long it took before he regained control. She was content to be the vessel giving an outlet for his grief.

When he finally raised his head, he gazed intently at her face inches from his and she brushed at the dampness where the sun glinted off the tears trapped in his beard.

"I've never done that before," he said wonderingly.

"Then it's time you did," she chided gently. "You don't get Brownie points for denying the relief tears can give."

His finger traced a path along the contour of her cheek, then across her eyebrow before trailing down her nose to outline the succulent curve of her mouth.

Something changed then between them, and her lips parted under the slight pressure he exerted. The wonderful warmth was building in her loins, spreading at an exciting rate, and she met his gaze, unabashed that her face was showing the same hunger disclosed in his.

Her eyes never left his as she captured his hand and kissed the padded tips of each finger in an erotic ritual, thrilling as the fire in their depths leaped into bright flames.

He shifted and she found herself on the sand. "Robyn!" Her name was a deep growl of desire in his throat as his mouth fastened on hers in a hungry search. There was no need for the usual foreplay; their bodies were already in tune to each other. Their mating was swift and explosive, yet Robyn felt a subtle

difference. It was as if what they had experienced
before had been the foundation and now they could
build for the future.

She lay in deep contentment, her eyes closed
against the flitting shafts of sunlight filtering through
the waving palm fronds. Philip lay partially sprawled
across her, his head cushioned between her breasts.
The even rate of his warm breath whispering across
her love-dampened skin told that he'd been able to
relax into sleep.

When had it happened? she wondered. When had
she lost her highly vaunted control and fallen in love?
The truth exploded in her with startling clarity. She
loved this man.

She made no attempt to dispute the fact. A deep
peace filled her as she at last accepted what her heart
had known but her mind had kept in abeyance. Her
hand stilled its light caresses along the long curve of his
back while she let the glory of the revelation blossom
and grow until every corner of her being glowed with
the knowledge.

At twenty-nine, she'd long ago decided she'd never
experience that special love she'd read about in
books, had even doubted its existence. She'd been
content with the controlled experiences she'd permitted. How could she have known it was possible to
respond to one man's hands with this total abandonment, to touch the stars with such a magnificent
explosion of passion?

Her breath quickened as her body recalled its
awakening. But what she felt went beyond their
physical mating. Their conversation proved their
minds met with the same blending. They both knew

the art world, knew many of the same people, and while they didn't always agree about the various artists, they respected each other's opinions.

Yes, things could work out when they returned to the States, she admitted with rising pleasure. She blinked her eyes as reality intruded, shattering her dream into a thousand pieces. Philip, while being a tremendous lover, had made no profession of love. While he'd shown he was fascinated by her mind and body, there'd been no indication he was interested in her heart.

Also, he had shown no inclination to leave this island; in fact, his every act had indicated that he intended to remain here. What was the answer, then? she asked herself. Was this newly discovered love strong enough to keep her here with him? Even as she considered the possibility, she wondered how long before this lotus-eating life would pall and her resentment would rise.

Philip had come here as an escape and in an effort to come to grips with his impending blindness. She couldn't fault him for doing that, but she had no driving reason to run from her previous life. It had given her great satisfaction, and while its importance had faded under this new awakening, she knew it would probably reassert its dominance.

Robyn had always been honest with herself. She'd always been a doer, and while she was enthralled at this time by the wonder of discovering this man and his habitat, she knew in her heart that eventually it wouldn't be enough. If Philip refused to return with her, she knew it would be better to leave before this

wonderful love became tarnished by her own restlessness.

Now what? she agonized. How was she going to
cope with her decision? The answer came slowly
through painful reflection. She had a week left. If she
took it one day at a time and drained each hour of its
pleasure, she'd have a storehouse of memories to
draw upon when she went through the readjustment
on her return home. She had never lost in the game of
love before and had only a bare inkling of the
wretchedness to be endured, but she sensed it would
be formidable. But she was a survivor, she consoled
herself stoically, and this was one game that was worth
whatever penalties she had to pay later.

Philip stirred, his lashes brushing her breast as he
woke to the realization of where he was. "What a
delightful pillow," he said, as he shifted to kiss each
soft mound before rising to his feet. She examined his
face hungrily, thrilled to find the torment gone.

"Come," he ordered, reaching for her hand. "I
think a swim is necessary to get rid of this sand."

The memories start now, she warned herself, and
rose to place a flirting kiss on his lips. They laughed as
they ran like two carefree children into the warm water
with Baylor barking in happy accompaniment by their
side.

10

~~~~~~~~~~~~~

Robyn hurried to meet Serina when she saw her emerge from the path. She was balancing two newly stretched canvases on her head, and when she left the protection of the trees, the breeze coming off the lagoon threatened to lift them from their precarious position.

"Pappa Nia found several boards that had drifted in and is splitting them to make more stretchers," the dark-skinned girl informed her.

"That's good," Robyn said. "I only hope his paint holds out until the supply ship arrives." She stilled the ache the thought gave her. When that happened, her stay would be over.

"I've never seen him paint so fast," Serina said in wonder when they reached the house and she saw the number of completed paintings lining the wall as the oils slowly hardened.

A small frown creased Robyn's brow after the girl left. She'd wondered about Philip's production. Following the day when he'd told her his story, he had worked as if driven. As long as there was enough light, he was at his favorite place on the beach creating glorious sweeps of color on a succession of canvases, each one taking her breath away with the soaring emotions they triggered in her.

She had assumed in her love that with the stirring emotions they shared, he was driven to express himself on canvas. There certainly was no hint of a depression, but now she wondered if his sight was still deteriorating as he'd intimated. Was he rushing to produce all he could in the precious time left to him?

As she was learning to do, she banished the depressing thought from her mind. The day was sultry, with a slight haze clouding the sky, and she wondered if there'd be rain that afternoon. Deciding on a swim, she untied her sarong and paused for a moment to admire her golden tan before running to the water's edge with a glorious sense of freedom.

The waves were high and they tumbled her about as she laughed at her helplessness. She emerged finally, gasping happily for breath as she marveled over the startling reversal of her attitude. Was she the same person who a little more than a week ago had been afraid of going in the water beyond her ankles? Who would have been appalled over running down the beach in the nude?

The relaxing of her inhibitions had been made possible through Philip. He'd made her proud of her body, made her vibrantly aware of her femininity, and his tenderness had opened her heart to the wonderful miracle of love.

Robyn glanced at Philip by his easel, her heart bursting with the need to express her love for him. She'd shown it in every way she could, but had never said the words, unsure of the depth of his own involvement.

Could a man indulge in such an exquisite sharing without love? She didn't know. During the moments of passion, they'd exchanged love words, but never had he said "I love you"—those three words that indicated commitment. As a result, she couldn't either, but she promised herself she would on the day she left. The gift would be left with him to ignore or to do with as he wished.

As she moved up the beach, she saw him frown as he glanced up at the sky. A frightening expression tightened his face as he bent to put his paints away. To her the daylight was still bright. But now she wondered if his sight had regressed so that even this pearly overcast was enough to affect his painting. The evidence hit her like a blow—he wouldn't have stopped if he could still see.

She dressed hurriedly and went to help him carry back his equipment. "It looks like we're in for some rain," she said brightly, hoping he'd think the sky was darker than it was.

Philip didn't answer as they trudged through the sand, but the deep lines bracketing his mouth showed he wasn't being fooled, that he was well aware of the bitter truth. When he left afterward to walk the beach, he didn't extend the usual invitation for her to go with him. Robyn watched with tear-stung eyes until he disappeared beyond their private cove, leaving her with the picture painfully engraved in her heart of the dejection depicted in every line of his magnificent golden body. Baylor, ever sensitive to his master's moods, padded silently by his side, his body brushing periodically against the long striding legs as if offering reassurance.

The sky kept its promise, and a few hours later, when the threatening clouds, heavy with rain, came rolling in from the ocean, Robyn sat anxiously in the doorway waiting for Philip's return. When the rains finally descended in their usual torrential downpour, she became frantic. Had something happened to him? Had he perhaps slipped on the treacherous coral outcroppings that she'd discovered lay exposed beyond the bend? Had Baylor elected to remain by his master instead of coming for her? Or worse, had Philip decided to swim away his frustration as was his habit, not realizing how much rougher the sea was now?

He finally appeared through the rain, thoroughly drenched, just as her screaming nerves demanded she take action. Her surge of relief was so intense that she couldn't move for several seconds. Then the reaction exploded within her.

"What do you mean by this senseless exposure?" she scolded. "Are you trying for pneumonia? How do you think we'd be able to get help to this godforsaken island?"

He stood under the sheltering roof extension, offering no excuse. Seeing him shiver, Robyn turned with an exasperated noise and stalked to the bed to pull off the thin blanket. She returned to wrap it around him after unfastening his dripping sulu. He remained passive as she briskly rubbed his hair dry with the edge of the blanket while continuing to berate him.

"You know why," he said in a peculiarly lifeless voice which cut through her remonstrations.

Robyn sucked in her breath on seeing the lost expression on his face, and her heart cried. "Yes," she whispered, knowing it was senseless to try to falsely minimize the ghastly truth.

He went unresistingly when she pulled him to the bed. She sat beside him when he lay down, and cradled him gently in her arms, murmuring little sounds that weren't words but told how she shared his new agony.

When he loosened her sarong, she lay down beside him, willingly offering her body with a tender encompassing love, knowing that this was one way to give him relief from the encroaching horror of total blindness that was creeping ever nearer. If their act of love could give him solace, she'd gladly be the healer.

Afterward, she was the one to gather him close and pillow his head on her breasts. Her hands moved in soothing caresses over the muscular curve banding his back, urging him to relax into a sleep that would give a few more precious moments of forgetfulness.

Philip's nap was short, but when he awoke, he was content to remain in the circle of her arms. "What do I do now, Robyn?" he agonized. "I suddenly discovered I wasn't able to tell the difference between the deeper blues and greens."

She screwed her eyes shut to deny the tears. "You were successful in changing your style once. Couldn't you do it again?"

He gave a short bitter laugh. "What do you suggest,

a series done in black and white until I have to throw away my brush? At the rate I'm slipping, that day isn't too far away. Of course, I could always take up weaving baskets. I'm sure Pappa Nia would be happy to arrange for some of the women to teach me."

"Don't," she whispered, his biting remark tearing at her with its bitterness. It was the agonizing of an artist realizing that his talents would soon have no outlet. She knew that when that happened the vital part of him that made Philip Holt so special would die, leaving only the shell of the man.

No! A fierce rebellion surged through her and her arms tightened around him protectively. Her gaze swept the room as she searched for inspiration. This was no time to mumble senseless platitudes; he was a man wrestling with his soul. He needed direction.

As if drawn by a magnet, her gaze fell on the wooden candlestick sitting on the table. She recalled the lovely carving he'd made of Baylor.

Robyn grasped his hand and brought it to her mouth to kiss each finger. "You have gifted hands," she said slowly, wondering how he'd take her suggestion. "You also have a God-given talent for creating beauty. There are other ways to give expression to your creativity."

She felt his body stiffen and draw slightly away as if he were building a protective barrier around himself, and she hurried into her explanation.

"I was admiring the candlestick you carved, and Serina showed me the carving you made of Baylor. Like all that you do, it had the Philip Holt stamp on it."

He flung himself from the bed, and she flinched on seeing him rigid with anger. "I admit carving candlesticks is one step above weaving baskets," he threw at her caustically. "I daresay there might be a market for them with the tourists who flock to Fiji."

"Don't be absurd," she returned stiffly, hurt by his misinterpretation of her suggestion. "What's wrong with working with wood? With the right tools you're bound to be superb. There are other media you can try—stone, that new plasteline, clay. There are so many that you're sure to find one that you can work with," she pressed eagerly, warming to her subject.

"Now you're insulting me by having me make mud pies!" he spat out in disgust as he whipped his sulu from the hamper and stomped out of the bure. The rain had moved on and he disappeared down the beach, his dog a dark shadow beside him.

Robyn huddled on the bed until her own anger surfaced. So much for permitting herself to be upset by his soul-destroying dilemma, she ranted silently to herself. She'd been a fool to let down her reserve so that he could hurt her this way. That Philip had been able to bring her alive to the full meaning of what being a woman meant simply indicated how expert he was in the art of seduction. She'd been nothing more than an available woman, one who'd capitulated without a murmur whenever he found the time to concentrate his admittedly considerable charm on her. Caught up in a girlish, romantic daydream of the ultimate hideaway with a virile man on a tropical island, she'd erroneously labeled her feelings as love when they were simply an infatuation, a result of their unexpected situation.

Robyn willfully erased all memory of the wonderful

afternoon on the beach when they'd shared tears and love. She put aside all the tender moments they'd had, the laughing times, the stimulating exploration of each other's minds.

She was tired of being vulnerable, of losing control over her actions. She'd been responding by instinct to each of Philip's many moods, subjugating her feelings to his. Somewhere along the line Robyn Stuart had become lost and it was time to resurrect her. She could understand and sympathize with the agony Philip must be going through, but that didn't give him the right to react so vehemently to her suggestions, to what had, after all, been a response to his question.

She was still certain that with time he could become a superlative sculptor. She'd seen what those wonderful, sensitive fingers could do. A thin cry escaped as she collapsed back on the pillow, her body reminded of the searching magic of those same fingers.

The atmosphere was still strained between them the next morning when she prepared breakfast. They both welcomed Serina's arrival with relief when she surprised them with an early appearance.

"Pappa Nia sent me to warn you that the freighter will be here this afternoon," she said apologetically while sending Robyn a woman's glance of sympathy.

Robyn gave a start of surprise. Surely the two weeks weren't up! "Is he certain?" she asked, surprised by her hope that there'd been an error. Hadn't she come to the conclusion during the night as they lay on opposite sides of the bed that she refused to become further involved in Philip's problems, that her one desire was to return to her previous, structured life so she could banish all memory of this accident of fate that had brought her here?

"Pappa always knows," Serina said with certainty.

Robyn's gaze fastened on Philip, but his head was lowered over his plate and she couldn't read his expression. She noticed, however, that his hands had stilled and his knuckles had become white around his coffee mug.

He finally raised his head and looked toward Serina. "Did you make a list of provisions I'll need? I daresay we ate into my spare stock these past few days."

"Yes, I thought of that," Serina replied with a sweet smile. "But I did want to check with you if you'd need any extra paint."

His chair scraped back as he rose quickly and strode to the door. He stared out over the lagoon for a long minute before he answered tonelessly, "No, I won't."

Serina's dark eyes darted questioningly between the two as if wondering about the strained atmosphere. "We'll be there waiting at the beach to say goodbye," she said shyly to Robyn.

"Will you come for her when you see the boat arriving?" Philip asked, his back still toward them.

Serina looked at him, startled. "Why, yes, if you wish me to."

Robyn could say nothing as the puzzled girl left. Occasionally they'd walked to the little settlement in the evening, so she was sure Philip knew the path well even in the dark. He evidently had no intention of doing the expected by going with her for this last farewell. Was his anger from the day before that strong that it canceled out all the other days and all they'd shared?

"If you like, you can select any painting you want to take with you when you go," he said in the carefully guarded voice he'd used since awakening.

Robyn stiffened over the tone of clear dismissal. "As payment for favors rendered?" she cried bitterly over the pain coursing through her.

His broad shoulders gave a negligible shrug. "Whatever. It's yours, though, not for that damned Cornell Gallery!"

She fought the desire to throw something at his unyielding back. Didn't he have the decency to at least face her as he attempted to pay her off as if she'd been nothing more than a kept woman?

She might be a salesperson, but the past two weeks had made her see him and his work in a different light. Somehow, selling his paintings had lost its importance in the wonder of what had been developing between them.

Developing? Her lips curled down under the force of her bitterness.

"I'll say goodbye now," Philip said without turning. He whistled for Baylor and stepped out into the sunshine. Robyn watched helplessly with a deepening shock as he once again disappeared down the beach, only this time he was walking out of her life.

11

Hazy pictures of the past twelve hours kept rolling before her mind's eye as Robyn prepared to leave. The shock produced by Philip's cruel rejection numbed her as she went mechanically through her usual morning chores.

In this bed she'd experienced the ultimate in bliss, one part of her cried, as she placed the mattress outside for its usual airing. After her quick sluicing, she dressed in the suit she'd worn on that fateful day when she'd walked innocently into Philip Holt's life and collapsed at his feet. Her body felt immediately smothered as it was totally covered for the first time since he'd introduced her to the freedom of the island's form of dress.

Checking stoically that she'd left everything in order, her eyes misted for a second on seeing that while her life had changed radically here, no imprint remained to tell of her passing. Her gaze wandered for one last time over the pictures lining the wall. Whoever had the honor of handling them should reap a fortune for his gallery as well as for Philip. At least he would have no money problems for life.

She looked at the picture he'd started after their first act of love. While she had entertained no intention of being paid off with the selection of a painting, she realized now that she couldn't let anyone else have that one. It was too expressive of their time together— at least until he'd turned bitter and, what was more painful, apparently denied what they had shared.

When it was evident that Philip had indeed said his final goodbye, she didn't wait for Serina to come for her. She struggled down the path alone, her painting wrapped carefully with the two sarongs.

Somehow she survived the boat ride back to Nadi. On arriving at the hotel, she found her luggage stored as Philip had predicted, plus several messages from Winslow.

"A Mr. Cornell called and we explained that you'd gone to Yagatiki and that there was no way we could get a message there," the desk clerk informed her. "He asked that you please call when you got back."

She thanked him but had no intention of returning Winslow's call. She'd gotten this far wrapped safely in her protective numbness, and the thought of reporting on even the surface happenings of the past two weeks was more than she could bear. Her most urgent need was to return to her apartment and lock the door behind her before the numbness wore off and she was exposed to the pain she knew lay waiting just below the surface.

The hotel clerk located a man who promised to have the large canvas boxed in time for her midnight flight, and she took a room so that she could indulge in the luxury of a long bath.

When she left the hotel, her facade was once again in place. She was Robyn Stuart, the chic, cool art connoisseur, in all outward respects in full control of her life. The rumpled suit had been left in a heap on the bathroom floor.

When she stepped into her apartment, Robyn felt strangely out of synch. Its svelte sophistication grated harshly on senses still attuned to the bure's tones of warm wood and textured matting, which blended harmoniously with the surrounding land. The dried pampas grass was an affront to her memories of waving palms and the ever-changing blues of the lagoon.

No! She struggled to hold back the surfacing agony. She mentally closed herself away from everything but the need to let her exhausted body collapse and find oblivion in sleep.

"That tan makes you look like a million!" Winslow exclaimed in admiration when she arrived at the gallery the next day. "You'll have to get a sun lamp to make sure it doesn't fade."

The smile that touched Robyn's lips never reached her eyes. She had intended to go through her accumulation of mail and restock her kitchen and not come in to work, but after glancing at one letter and not comprehending what she was reading, she knew she had to escape before memories came crashing down on her. Even facing Winslow's questions was better than the solitude of empty rooms that had never heard Philip's rich baritone laughter; of looking at chairs that never felt the imprint of wide bronzed shoulders; and, God help her, of a bed that never knew the magic of their love.

"Now tell me, what success have you had with Holt?" Winslow's eyes were bright with anticipation now that the formality of greeting was over.

"No more than you had," she returned with a surprisingly even voice as she braced herself for the inquisition.

His face registered an incredulous skepticism. "You mean you spent two weeks on the island with that man and didn't get a commitment of any kind?"

"You forget he already has an agent. Marshall in San Francisco always handled him." She'd never had the courage to bring up the subject after Philip's first vitriolic denunciation, or try to further Winslow's case.

A dusky color stained Winslow's neck and rose to his ears as his lips thinned with barely suppressed anger. "What in the devil did you do for those two weeks that you neglected to make contact with me? I assumed you must have been having some difficulties and needed the extra time. After all, I'd met him and seen how obstinate he could be. Now you're telling me the time was wasted?"

Wasted? She would have laughed if she hadn't felt so close to crying. "You were there and saw how difficult it is to get to the out islands. The plane you used had engine problems, so I had to take an island ferry to get there. It wasn't until it was too late that I found out that it wouldn't return for two weeks. And, in case you didn't know, there was no radio communication available."

"You mean you were stranded and couldn't get off?" Winslow's face held a moment's sympathy as his fastidious nature shuddered at the idea of having to endure such a catastrophe. "I saw those huts the natives live in. You poor thing, how did you ever manage to survive?"

She suppressed her sigh of relief. She wasn't about to correct his impression. If he believed she'd stayed in the small compound, it obliterated the need to side-step around the truth. "I found out one can do anything if one's forced to," she answered obliquely. "And I'm truly sorry that I couldn't bring you better news. As you suspected, Philip Holt can be a very obstinate man." How obstinate, he'd never know.

Winslow sat on the corner of his desk, a frown of annoyance darkening his face. "I'm in a quandary. I was holding the painting I brought back with me, figuring you'd bring more so I could have a show of his new work. I'd be able to place a much higher price on them if the public was confident that this was the way he was going and that it wasn't just a solitary effort."

Robyn's attention was caught by the nervous tattoo of Winslow's manicured fingers on the desk, and it struck her with breath-stopping force that she was again locked into the world of smartly attired and manicured people that sulus and sarongs and carefree diving into crystal-clear water in the buff was the world that would soon fade into unreality.

"The painting is good enough alone to demand a

considerable price," she offered, knowing of several clients who'd be more than happy to add a Philip Holt to their collection. She recalled the magnificent sweep of colors that had started the first rumblings that had shaken her world, and she wondered with a fierce desire for ownership if her own bank account could afford it.

"You're right, of course," Winslow agreed with a sigh for lost profits. But he wasn't one to waste time on the unattainable. "The first shipment has just arrived from the Philippines," he said, his expression brightening. "I'm starting to uncrate them in the back room. Come and tell me what you think of Ramon Torquez's technique."

The tension drained from Robyn. She'd been anxious about the grilling she feared she'd have to go through from an irate Winslow for the failure of her mission. She didn't doubt that there'd be more questions later, but the worst was over.

She followed him to give her input on his latest acquisitions, thankful for the reprieve.

They were very good, and when they decided to hold a show in the near future, Robyn welcomed the work. She threw herself completely into the project. Photos had to be taken of the oils, and the catalogue had to be printed. The layout of the adjustable screens had to be decided upon so that the colorful impressionistic paintings were shown to their best advantage. The caterer was contacted, and to keep in the mood of the exotic flamboyance of Torquez's subjects, she decided to be innovative and offer ethnic foods. There was also considerable time put into persuading the reluctant artist to fly in for the show. It seemed he'd never been on a plane before and he had to be cajoled into coming.

By the time the show was ready, Robyn was close to complete exhaustion. Winslow eyed her critically when they were giving their final inspection to the gallery.

"I know you've been pushing yourself hard to pull this all together on such short notice, but I've never seen you look so terrible," he said bluntly. "You'd better take a few days off when this is all over."

Free time was the last thing Robyn wanted. She'd welcomed the demanding work, involving herself in every detail instead of delegating some of it to Gretchen. It had helped stop the invasion of memories during the day, but there'd been nothing to still the dreams that descended at night. She'd even resorted to trying sleeping pills, but they left her with a nagging headache. When she did collapse from exhaustion, the sleep didn't refresh her and she'd drag herself to the gallery the next day, hoping that by working even harder she'd eventually find a level at which her senses would become numb.

The show was a sellout, and the artist, dazed by his success, was sent home to produce more while he was still a hot item.

Winslow, smugly satisfied over having been astute enough to see Torquez's potential, was eager to capture more budding artists for his gallery. He was obviously pleased with his growing stature in the art world as a discoverer of new talent.

"I've decided to go east next week to see what's available in Cape Cod," he told Robyn when the last painting had been crated and sent to its new owner. "As you know, it's a mecca for artists every summer, and with autumn soon upon us I think it's smart to look them over before most of them disperse."

Robyn agreed, her attention only partly on what he was saying as she went through the mail that had just arrived. The last time he'd gone there he'd found some minor work that had eventually sold.

"And, Robyn," he added as he leaned over her desk, "perhaps when I return you won't be so tired." He tapped her cheek gently before turning to answer his telephone and didn't see the color flushing her cheeks.

She knew what he was alluding to. The week before, she'd accepted a dinner date with him and afterward had invited him to her apartment. He'd been there often enough, but this time she had asked him with the full intention of ending the evening in bed. She'd come to the conclusion that one way to exorcise the haunting presence of a bearded man was to replace it with another. Winslow was her choice. After all, hadn't she decided on that long-ago day when Winslow had returned from his trip to Fiji that he would be an acceptable lover?

But the evening hadn't ended as planned. She could muster only a tepid response to Winslow's kisses, and when he had looked at her questioningly, she had used the excuse of being exhausted from the long hours she'd put in to ready the show.

It was later, curled on her lonely bed, that she accepted the fact that once having experienced the wonder of Philip Holt's arms, it was impossible to consider lying in anyone else's. Until time helped to dim the ache his memory always precipitated, she was fated to go her lonely way.

The day before he was to leave, Winslow tossed a newspaper clipping on her desk. "I came across this in a Laguna Beach paper and thought that if you can find some free time while I'm gone, you could follow up on it."

Robyn glanced over the half sheet of newsprint devoted to a Roland Fleming, a local artist who was having a small show. Her heart gave an uncomfortable lurch when she examined the accompanying photo. He was tall with a dark beard, and unwanted memories clamored for attention. He stood with attempted nonchalance by one of his paintings. It depicted a little girl sitting primly on the edge of a Victorian sofa, and she saw immediately what had prompted Winslow's interest. The black-and-white photo gave no hint of the colors used, but the delicate handling of the way the child was positioned indicated a sensitivity that caught the viewer's attention.

"I'll make the time on Sunday," she promised, immediately liking what she saw.

The gallery closed early on Saturday, and Robyn spent the rest of the day browsing through a nearby mall. She was finding it more and more difficult to return to her apartment. She used to find peace in its cool austerity, but now she kept pacing the floor and rearranging the furniture, driven by a discontent and restlessness that followed her even to bed.

Time, Robyn kept reminding herself in despair, would heal her never-ending ache and solve the restlessness. To help it pass, she drove herself constantly, searching for projects to fill the empty periods away from the gallery.

Sunday was always the most difficult day, and she was thankful for Winslow's request. She breakfasted on juice and a cup of black coffee, her usual spartan fare. Breakfasts were no longer a shared event.

With a cry that rose from the painful memories that refused to fade, Robyn grabbed her purse and hurried from her apartment. Once in her car, she was forced to give her attention to the traffic and the intricacies of reaching the highway that led south and to the beach road. The article had stated the show would be open on Sunday afternoon, and she hoped there'd be an adequate sample of the artist's work so she could decide if he were worth approaching.

The gallery was indeed small. The main business of the proprietor was picture framing, and as an adjunct to his business he evidently permitted the store's front room to be used by unrecognized artists as a place to display their work.

On entering, she saw only two people examining the paintings on the walls. Her attention, however, fastened on the tall, lanky man leaning with unconcerned ease against the counter at the back of the store, and she recognized Roland Fleming from the photo.

He paused in his conversation with the woman sitting behind the counter and examined Robyn with lingering care from under a questioning, cocked eyebrow.

Her heart rate leaped at the shock of seeing him. At first glance he looked so much like Philip that she hadn't been able to keep the hunger from showing.

The differences were immediately noted, but she knew he'd seen that first unguarded look, and she turned to the paintings to hide her embarrassment.

He was younger than Philip—closer to her own age. There were no silver touches to his dark hair and his eyes were blue instead of a near ebony. Yet the way he held his head was achingly reminiscent of the way Philip had.

She had moved along one full wall before realizing she hadn't seen one of the paintings. She took a deep breath and forced her attention on her reason for being here.

Most of the paintings were portraits, and she saw that he was exceptionally good. The skin tones were not as superb as those Philip had been capable of producing, nor did he have Philip's perceptions, but she couldn't fault him on technique and use of color. Winslow had few good portrait artists in his stable, and acquiring Roland Fleming would be advantageous.

When she'd finished, she walked over to him, nursing a suspicion that he'd been watching her every move as she evaluated each portrait.

"Mr. Fleming?" she asked, handing him her card. "I'm Robyn Stuart."

He straightened slowly, a sharp interest lighting his eyes on reading the name printed on the card. The Cornell Gallery was well known among artists, its reputation one of the best in the area.

"Do you have any more examples of your work, and can we go someplace where we can talk?" She watched with amusement as he tried to contain his rising excitement.

"My place is down on the beach," he volunteered with barely suppressed eagerness. "And I have paintings stacked in every corner!" He couldn't restrain the broad grin from emerging. "I also have a bottle of wine that a friend promised was exceptionally fine. I'd be pleased if you would give me your opinion of it."

He reminded her of a puppy dog unable to control his exuberance, and she found herself smiling her acceptance.

Robyn followed his battered van north until he finally left the highway before reaching Newport Beach. After a succession of narrowing roads, he stopped before a weathered cottage raised on posts so that one could see over the sand dunes to the ocean.

"I inherited it from an aunt, bless her soul," he said as he unlocked the door. "She was a frustrated artist and said it was her way of guaranteeing a roof over my head until I was discovered."

The furniture was shabby and nondescript, but the view that confronted her made that unimportant. Robyn went to the window as if drawn by a magnet. This was her first sight of the Pacific in two months, and she swallowed over the constriction in her throat. Far beyond the horizon sat a small island where this same blue water lapped in caressing waves on the beach. Was Philip Holt swimming in it with the faithful Baylor by his side? But more important, was he able to see any of the brilliant blues of the lagoon, or was his dependence on his dog complete?

Robyn blinked hard against the mist filming her eyes. Was she ever going to be free of this terrible sense of loss? She turned back to the room, determined not to let the pain intrude. Philip had rejected her but her life had to go on. She focused her attention on Roland Fleming.

"I'll have to remember the name of this wine," Robyn said as Roland portioned out the last of the bottle. It was three hours later and they were enjoying sharp cheddar cheese and black bread and drinking the rich ruby wine. It was a celebration of sorts. While Winslow would have to give his final approval, Robyn was certain he'd come to the same conclusion that she had. Roland Fleming had a great future before him.

From the lineup of paintings, she found at least a dozen that met the gallery's high standards and were good enough to show. Roland could hardly contain himself as he alternately sat in dazed disbelief and stalked the room in excited exuberance. She could appreciate the mixed emotions that he was experiencing. If Winslow decided to give his own stamp of approval with a show of his own, Roland could claim to have finally arrived.

He drained his glass and jumped up once more to stand before Robyn, an abashed grin making him look entrancingly boyish. "I know I'm acting like an adolescent, but this is more than I ever hoped for!" He ran a hand through hair already well rumpled. "Look, would you like to go for a walk?" he begged. "If I don't do something, I'll explode!"

Robyn smiled in sympathy, then raised a foot to show the thin-strapped high-heel sandals she wore. "I don't think these are exactly right for beachwear," she apologized. But she could understand his need, and suddenly she ached to follow his lead. It had been much too long since she'd felt the sand between her toes. "If I can use your bedroom to remove my hose?" she asked.

He agreed happily, and they soon were climbing over the dune and to the water's edge where the sand was firmer. They paused to roll up their pants to protect them from the reaching waves. She watched with indulgent humor as Roland jogged off a short distance, then returned to join her in a brisk walk.

The afternoon had been a pleasant experience. Except for that one flight into the past, she realized that somehow she'd been able to keep the invading memories at bay. Roland, she knew, had been partly the reason. She enjoyed his company. "Is the beach always this empty?" she asked as they matched strides.

"Fortunately, we're a distance from the public beach," he informed her. "It's only on weekends that the overflow comes this far."

There was no dark forest sweeping down to the beach, but something about the small cover had her looking around with a rising interest at the short row of identical houses peeking over the protective sand dune. Roland, seeing her inspection, explained how they were all put up by the same builder.

"They were built as speculation before this area became popular and are all laid out similarly to mine. Nothing fancy but very adequate. We're managing to hang on against the high-rises that are taking over everything."

She spotted a For Sale sign on one a few houses from his and found herself walking toward it.

"I heard the owners were thinking of leaving," he

said with a shrug of indifference. "I guess it's true. The sign wasn't there this morning."

They strolled around the building. From the cursory inspection it seemed sound. Robyn didn't need to look inside, as she could see that the layout was the same as Roland's. In her mind's eye she could visualize it decorated in earth tones accented with reds and yellows, with the warmth of polished wood and scatter rugs. There'd be no chrome and glass.

At that instant she knew she had to have the house, that the reason for her constant need to escape from her present apartment was because of its sterile austerity. Was that how she'd viewed her life before a man on a remote island had changed everything?

When Winslow returned from his trip, she told him about Roland Fleming. After viewing his work, he concurred with her evaluation of the artist's potential and arranged for a future showing.

Winslow wasn't as enthusiastic later when he heard of her moving. "Don't tell me you intend to go native!" he exclaimed, his face expressing his disbelief after he'd inspected her purchase. Winslow raised a speculative eyebrow when Roland arrived to put up the brackets for the curtains, but Robyn didn't say anything.

Over the months a warm affection had developed between them, but from the first, Robyn warned Roland frankly that he could hope for nothing more than friendship, and he wisely accepted the limits she set.

They spent long evenings walking the beach, where they talked lengthily on any and every subject that appealed to them. But most important he taught her to laugh again.

When it first happened, Roland stopped in mid-stride and stared wonderingly at her. "Do you know that's the first time you've done more than smile at something I've said? You're a beautiful woman, Robyn Stuart. It's about time you started enjoying yourself again."

Robyn averted her face from his questing look and gazed sadly at the waves breaking at their feet. Time had passed since she'd known Philip's love, and her aching sense of loss had diminished, but she knew she wasn't ready to start anything new. She knew she was being selfish, remaining friends with Roland when he obviously wanted to be more than a friend, but she had nothing more to offer.

Her tenuous control was shattered when she foolishly uncrated Philip's painting and her longing resurfaced with a crushing force. Since her return it had been kept out of sight, pushed to the back of a closet. At the time, she couldn't have faced the daily proof of the special enchantment that had been theirs. Philip might have been able to deny it later, but she was certain that the sensitive artist in him could never have depicted such explicit emotion unless he had felt it at the time. Holding to her conviction had been both her salvation and her torment.

The painting belonged over her fireplace, and the following day, convinced that she was finally mending, she hung it in the place of honor. Tears dampened her cheeks as she stood for long minutes before it—tears of regret for lost dreams, for a love that held no hope.

She looked around the large room, bright from the

windows lining three sides. She'd decorated her new home a room at a time, but since she had little need for the space, she'd left this room for last. In Roland's house, it was used as his studio, and for a heart-clutching moment she could visualize the floor littered with curls of wood and the shadowy forms of magnificent pieces of sculpture. She hurried from the room.

All evening the painting kept drawing her, beckoning her to explore memories best kept buried. No matter where she sat, or what she was trying to concentrate on, she invariably found herself standing before the glorious swirl of colors, experiencing anew its uplifting joy.

Why had it had to end? she thought in despair. What they'd been given had been so special! It had been special for him too. She knew that with a deep certainty. He might not have fallen in love as she had, but for those precious two weeks he'd been caught up in the exquisite beauty of what they'd shared.

They had met as equals at so many levels. They both knew the art world, and, seen from the different viewpoints of creator and seller, it had made for long hours of stimulating conversation. And their time in each other's arms . . . She sucked in her breath, remembering how each time had convinced them that this one was the ultimate experience, only to discover the next one surpassed it in intensity.

Robyn tossed restlessly in her bed, her flesh heating with a passion too long denied. "Philip, Philip!" She whispered his name into the night air, only to have it fade, an echo of longing for what might have been.

But it could be again, a small voice urged. All it would take was a plane ticket. For a moment Robyn envisioned their meeting. She could feel the sun's heat on her back, hear the rustle of the palm trees by his bure, smell the salt-laden breeze coming off the blue lagoon. And she could feel his strong arms close around her, his lips taking and draining her as only Philip's could.

No! she groaned. Her breath came in gasps as she wrenched herself from her fantasy. She'd been lucky to be given those two weeks. She'd become a better woman for the experience. It had broken her from the brittle world that she'd been content in, and she had to be thankful for that. Any fool knew one could never recapture what had once ended.

And it had ended. Philip had been very explicit that final day. If only they'd had time to resolve that last bitterness. She sighed with regret as the heat generated by the influx of memories slowly faded.

No, flying to Fiji would resolve nothing. The only thing it would settle was what direction Philip had taken. There would always be that lingering concern over what had become of Philip the artist, because how he handled that vital part of him determined what became of Philip the man.

Two days later, when she finished talking with a prospective purchaser at the gallery, she walked into Winslow's office. He was going through the mail that had arrived while she'd been occupied. He slit open a large envelope and pulled out a brochure. His mouth thinned as he glanced at the cover and tossed it to her across the desk.

"This is one show we have to go to even if it hurts," he said. "It looks like he's stayed with Marshall in San Francisco. They're having a showing of Philip Holt's latest work in two weeks, and they've enclosed two invitations to the preview.''

Shock waves tore through Robyn as she stared at the colored booklet. She struggled against the threatening black void that seemed to have opened at her feet.

12

The two weeks passed in torturous indecision. One minute Robyn would decide flatly that she wanted no reminder of Philip Holt to shake the relative peace she'd finally achieved. But the next she realized that that chapter of her life could never be closed until she went to the exhibit to see how he'd coped after she'd left. The need was imperative. There were too many unanswered questions that could only be resolved by going.

Had his sight had a remission so that he could continue with his paintings? If she saw any in black and white, she knew she'd die a little. A shudder ran through her as she recalled his scathing words.

It amazed her that Winslow seemed unaware of the emotions tearing at her. After all, he knew she'd spent two weeks on Philip's island. When Winslow hadn't followed his first questioning with anything further, she'd assumed it was because he was sensitive to her privacy. Did he assume that since she'd sidestepped his own advances her willpower had been strong enough to resist Philip's brand of virility? Resist! A bitter laugh rose to her lips. All Philip had to do was touch her and she'd become putty in his hands!

Roland was more sensitive to her turmoil. On one fog-shrouded evening when they walked the beach, it became easy under his gentle probing to tell him a part of what she'd been going through.

"You know you have to go," he said finally. "You owe it to yourself to go and see if, after inspecting his work, you can lay the ghost to rest."

He stopped to gather her in his arms. "You owe it to yourself . . . and to me. You must know how I feel about you. How long do you think I can remain content in the role you're forcing me to play?"

"Oh, Roland," she murmured contritely, pressing her cheek against his. He tilted her head back and kissed her. But even while he kissed her, she found herself comparing the tepid warmth she felt to the fire that had consumed her instantly when Philip's lips had touched hers.

Resenting the intrusion of the unwanted memories, she tried to infuse more enthusiasm into her kiss, but eventually she pulled away in dull despair. She was *acting* a response, not *living* it, and it wasn't fair to raise Roland's hopes. Yes, she had to go to San Francisco and see to ending the unwanted impasse Philip had placed on her emotions. It was senseless to behave as if there were nothing more to experience once having known Philip's love.

Two days before the event, it hit her that Philip

might be at the exhibit. She didn't know why she'd never considered it before, except that he'd been so adamant that he'd never leave his hideaway. What if he were there! The thought sent her senses into a tailspin, and at one point she started to dial the Marshall Gallery for confirmation. She stopped when she realized that she'd never have the courage to go if he were there, and by now some deep instinct told her that this trip was imperative.

A further blow came the next day when an incipient cold that Winslow had been nursing became full-blown, putting him to bed with a temperature of 102. Robyn knew she was acting the coward when she asked Roland if he'd accompany her instead.

He looked at her for a long thoughtful minute before telling her it was something she'd have to work out on her own. There was nothing he could do to help.

Robyn had to accept the reasoning behind his refusal. She boarded the plane by herself the following day, determined to resolve alone the hold Philip Holt had placed on her.

Growing anxiety blinded her to the attractive entrance of the hotel she signed in to. The preview reception wasn't until eight that night, and Winslow had wisely insisted that hotel reservations be made so that there'd be no need to cut short their attendance to catch the late shuttle back to L.A.

She had no appetite and had coffee and a Danish sent to her room before she showered and dressed in the blue cocktail dress she'd brought with her. Only when dressed did she remember that blue was the color of the outfit Philip had first seen her in, and she was unsettled by the feeling of *déjà vu*.

When the taxi deposited Robyn in front of the Marshall Gallery, she was a bundle of nerves. What in the world was she doing here? she questioned in rising panic.

Another taxi arrived and discharged two couples. Robyn drew in a calming breath before removing the engraved invitation card from her purse and following them into the brightly lit building. There was no need to act like an adolescent, she scolded herself.

She saw with satisfaction that the main room was already filled with people. It would be a simple matter to blend with the crowd, do what she came to do, and leave unobtrusively. A waiter paused before her, offering a glass of champagne from his tray. She accepted one, took a fortifying sip, and turned to the paintings on the wall.

The main room, she saw immediately, was devoted to Philip's portraits, loaned by proud owners. Examining them reaffirmed the fact that his fame had been well deserved. There'd been only one example shown in the brochure of his later work, and she looked around her, tension returning. It was her need to see how Philip was now managing to cope that had brought her here.

She saw an entrance to a side room and inched her way through the crowd. It was then she saw him, and she gave a strangled gasp, causing the man beside her to look at her with concern.

The group of people crowding around him had parted slightly and she saw Philip Holt holding court, sitting with negligible ease on a high stool. His teak-dark tan had faded, but his hair and beard were expertly trimmed, and she tried not to remember that long-ago enchanted afternoon when she'd cut his hair herself.

He was wearing brown shaded glasses, and she hoped passionately that medical knowledge had come up with a way to augment his remaining sight.

The gap closed and she somehow managed to continue into the adjoining room. Philip was here! Every nerve quivered over the wonder of seeing him once more. At that moment Robyn accepted that time had not cured her of her love for the man. It had only made its existence more bearable.

She had no idea how long she stood staring blindly at the painting she'd stationed herself in front of. Gradually the remarks of the people around her filtered through. It became evident that once they got over the shock of the whole new technique Philip had developed they were impressed with what they saw.

Her examination became a painful trip into the past. Now the paintings were attractively framed, but she remembered the effect they'd had on her when she'd lined them up outside his thatched hut. By the time she reached the ones he'd done when she'd been with him, she was trembling as memories that she'd thought were successfully buried sprang into renewed life as if they'd happened the day before.

Again she felt the gritty sand under her as she sat and watched Philip sweep the paint across the canvas. The sun was again a warm band on her back as the palm fronds waved lazily above her. And she heard the little grunt of satisfaction that Baylor always gave when he settled beside her to be stroked as they watched the man they both loved, lost in his private world.

The joyous swirls expressed on these canvases ended abruptly. The next two were composed of jagged lines that shouted their anger. Her hand pressed against her heart with the pain they triggered. Was this how he'd felt after she left? She hurried past them to the last one on display and she wondered why they had hung it. While well executed, it contained little of the fire or emotional impact the others imparted. It was composed of yellows and reds on a white background, and suddenly Philip's agonizing confession rang in her ears—that it had become increasingly difficult to distinguish between the darker colors. This, then, must have been his last painting, his swan song.

She turned away from it with tears in her eyes. What now? How was Philip, the artist, coping now that he'd lost this avenue of expressing himself? She shuddered, remembering their final morning together and his bitter words about weaving baskets.

Robyn stepped aside to permit several people to exit from another side room she hadn't noticed before. They were talking excitedly over what they had just viewed.

"He's remarkable, a truly gifted artist!" a smartly dressed woman exclaimed.

The man beside her nodded in quick agreement. "I understand there's pressure to send this show around the country."

Robyn glowed on hearing their positive reaction to Philip's work. She realized it was silly to feel this way, but she felt she was a part of Philip and therefore part recipient of any praise he received.

Evidently the room they'd just left held more of Philip's work, and she was interested to see if perhaps there was some of his earlier work from before he'd become famous. She'd often wondered about what he'd produced during those developing years.

She entered and stopped short in surprise. The room was bare except for three spotlighted pedestals. Each supported a piece of sculpture, and Robyn felt herself drawn to the largest one displayed in the center. Sheer joy invaded her as she realized that in spite of his words, he'd accepted her suggestion after all.

The wooden sculpture, half-life-size, was of a man and woman reclining. She was on her back and he was braced on one elbow, leaning partially over her. One of her hands rested on his shoulder, the other on his chest. While he cradled her head in one arm, his other curved around her body. The tenderness and passion explicit in every line of their bodies and lighting their faces told of the imminent act of love.

An uncontrollable tremor made it impossible for Robyn to move, for something deep inside her told her that she was that woman and the man was Philip. Memories flooded her of the way his sensitive hands had molded every inch of her as if programming his fingertips with her very essence, a programming that had made this interpretation possible.

When she was able to tear her eyes from the beauty of the polished wood, she turned in a trancelike state to the second pedestal. It was a bust molded in clay of a woman with her face raised slightly, a tender smile parting her lips.

Robyn's clasped hands went to her mouth to still

her cry as she recognized her own features. She was deeply moved by his sensitive rendition. If he'd seen that expression on her face so that by touch alone he could reproduce it, he must have been aware of her love. She'd always regretted not having told him as she'd planned, but it hadn't been necessary, not necessary at all.

She turned to the last stand. This, too, was in wood, and it was an almost life-sized rendition of Baylor. He'd often sat in that identical position, begging for a scratch behind the ear, and Robyn almost found her hand going out to oblige.

"Woof!" The soft sound was so much a part of the realism of the carving that it took a moment for Robyn to realize that a warm furry head was nudging her.

"He told me a half hour ago that you were here, but I had a difficult time getting away from the crowd." The deep voice with its unique cadence came from behind her, and Robyn turned to face the man her heart had never forgot.

"Philip!" she breathed in a trembling whisper.

"You've seen the others?" he asked, his voice deepening.

"Yes!" she answered. *Oh, yes, yes!* her heart echoed.

"We have a lot to talk about," he began, and frowned in annoyance when several people entered the room, giving exclamations of surprise over seeing the sculpture.

"Let's get out of here," he said brusquely. "I've had enough people to last me a long time. There's a back way that we take." His hand brushed her shoulder as he searched for her arm, and he urged her into the other room before anyone could recognize him and stop him.

"The way to the stockroom is somewhere off here," he said impatiently, and Robyn led him to the closed door, biting her lip as she realized his frustration over his inability to locate it.

Before Robyn could absorb the miracle of seeing Philip again, they were out in the alley, skirting the caterer's van parked there, and into a taxi they were fortunate to find waiting there for a fare.

Only then did Philip release the tight hold he'd maintained on her arm, as if he'd been afraid that she might disappear on him.

"Where are you staying?" he asked, and when she gave him the name of the hotel, he passed it on to the driver before settling back in the seat. He found her hand and held it pressed against his thigh. "We'll go there," he said with satisfaction. "Marshall will no doubt send someone to my place when he finds I'm gone, and I don't want any interruptions. We have too much to discuss."

How true, she agreed. There were a lot of questions that needed answers, but somehow they didn't seem so important now with him sitting so close to her, their shoulders and hips touching. A myriad of tingling signals were set off by the movement of his thigh under her hand.

By the time they entered the hotel, she was beyond coherent thought. The clerk behind the desk looked askance at the large black dog, but made no objection as they went to the elevator. For the first time Robyn noticed the special seeing-eye harness Baylor was wearing and wondered how the animal was tolerating its restriction and the confusion of life in a city after the freedom he'd enjoyed on the island.

With the release of Philip's hold, Robyn was able to regain partial control over her emotions. There remained no doubt in her that her love for this man was as strong as ever, but she'd suffered through his rejection once and had survived the months of pain. She'd managed to rebuild her life brick by painful brick. Was she supposed to let him enter it again, only to suffer the agony of a second rejection when his unpredictable mood had him denying her once more? He said there was much to discuss, and she agreed heartily.

She unlocked the door to her room and crossed the shag carpet to drop her purse on the dresser. After drawing in a controlling breath in an effort to marshal her thoughts into a protective shield, she turned to him. Her poise shattered immediately into tiny shards upon seeing him standing uncertainly in the middle of the room, obviously not knowing where to move. He'd released Baylor, and the dog was sniffing the corners of the room.

"You'll have to help me, Robyn," he said with a quiet dignity that told of his hard-won acceptance of his fate. "I can only see vague shadows."

She knew he was waiting for her to go to him, and it took all of her willpower not to succumb to the need to have his arms around her once again. "There's a chair about four feet to your left if you wish to sit down," she directed, respecting the independence that had always been an integral part of him.

"Have I hurt you that much?" he asked in a low voice. "I can only say that I've suffered more." When she didn't answer, he moved slowly until he made contact with the chair.

He sat hunched forward with his hands clasped, his elbows braced on his knees. He stared at the floor between them for a long minute as if searching for the right words with which he hoped to bridge their separation. "I have a lot to ask your forgiveness for," he admitted. "I'm not proud of my actions the day you left. I can only hope I can help you to understand why I was driven to act the way I did."

He glanced up, but when she made no comment, he had no sound to focus on and his eyes dropped once more to the rug. "My sight loss had been in a state of remission for about a year. Then, after Winslow Cornell left, I noticed a further dimming. When you arrived, literally dropping at my feet, I'd been in a black despair. It's impossible to describe how I felt the next morning after having spent the night with you in my arms. I realized then how desperately I needed the touch of another human. I never planned to take advantage of you, but you were so warm and responsive, I could no more have stopped what happened than fly. At first, I hated myself for taking what you offered so freely, but being in your arms soon became a necessity to me. It helped to keep at bay the burden of fear over what the future held."

His shoulders twitched as if he'd been holding them taut too long, and he leaned back in the chair and closed his eyes before continuing. "I'll never forget that last afternoon on the beach. I knew I loved you then."

An inarticulate cry was smothered as Robyn was swept with the sweet memory of their shared tears and tender love. It had been then that she, too, had admitted the full scope of her feelings for him to herself. But if he had experienced the same revelation, it made the reason for his later rejection even more incomprehensible.

Her heart was willing to forgive, but memories of the desolation she'd suffered in lonely despair through the ensuing months bound her to her chair.

Philip removed his glasses and dropped them in his pocket before brushing his hand across his eyes in a weary gesture. Hearing no answer from her, his face slackened in an expression of defeat but he continued doggedly with his confession.

"I was all tied into knots. Our time together was running short, and while the thought of your leaving was almost more than I could bear, the new evidence that my sight was deteriorating at a much faster rate was even worse. What did I have to offer a woman, especially one of your caliber? The comfort of money, yes; my portraits had made me wealthy. But I was afraid of the person I thought I would become when I no longer could find expression for this driving force in me that needs to have an outlet."

Philip halted again and Robyn sensed that he was waiting for her to speak. Ever since they'd been in the room, she'd been aware of the tension sparking between them, of the nearly uncontrollable need to touch. The passionate part of her that he'd brought to life was urging her to answer the siren call, to once again soar in the magic of his arms. But the pain of his past rejection held her back.

"Your sculptures are outstanding," she said, breaking into the silence.

"I'm surprised at how much I enjoy working with wood and clay," Philip admitted, taking her lead. "Have you heard of Sigler? He's one of the best sculptors in America, I think. When I contacted him a month after you left, he honored me by letting me work with him in his studio near Newport Beach. He's a tough teacher, but he helped me refine my own technique." A grim smile touched his lips, telling of harsh lessons learned.

Robyn was momentarily speechless under the shock of discovering that he'd left the island a month after she had and had been mere miles away from her beach house all that time. A bitterness curled in her over the fact that he'd made no attempt to contact her. So much for his confession of love!

The silence lengthened between them as Robyn struggled with her emotional uncertainties. Then Philip broke the awkward impasse. "I've taken enough of your time, Robyn," he said with a quiet resignation. "Thank you for giving me the opportunity to talk with you." He rose and stood for a second, shifting his shoulders as if testing the balance of an intolerable weight.

Baylor positioned himself by his master and Robyn stood stiffly to one side to let them pass. She'd given of herself unconditionally to this man, and it hurt unbearably to hear his admission that he'd used her as a bulwark to help ward off the panic brought on by his increasing blindness. But yet . . . but yet . . .

Through his work, Philip had let her know that he loved her. Hadn't he spent the past year creating in loving detail that sculpture depicting the response they'd shared during so many sun-kissed days and star-filled nights? The exquisite tenderness of the emotion expressed by the two carved figures should tell her of the depth of his declaration. Why then this reluctance to accept the truth of his words? Did she need to inflict on him some of the suffering she'd gone through?

She watched him walk by, his head bowed in acceptance. Where was the remembered firm thrust of his legs when he'd strode alongside her on the beach, the proud lift to his head that had been emblazoned in her heart since that first meeting? Who was she punishing so blindly—Philip or herself? Had she learned nothing from that parched existence without him during the past year?

"Philip." His name was a weak whisper forced through the spasm closing her throat.

He hesitated in his search for the doorknob. "It's all right, Robyn," he answered with a weary shrug. "I can understand your inability to forgive me. I let it go too long because of my damned pride in having to prove myself. Besides, there's no earthly reason for you to want to have anything further to do with me."

Robyn caught her breath, realizing what the bitterness in his voice was inferring. Did he think that his blindness was the reason behind her rejection? It had never occurred to her that he might think that made any difference to her, any more than the loss of a leg would have done. Yes, she loved his physical masculinity; but even more, she loved the inner essence of him that made him so special to her.

Anger rose in her at herself for letting him harbor that belief. The overwhelming compassion, the full swell of her love melted her frozen limbs and she went swiftly to his side. Her hand covered his, stilling the turning of the doorknob.

"Philip Holt, you're out of your mind if you think I'll let the man I love walk out of my life a second time!" she cried breathlessly.

Robyn understood the tremor running through him. It matched her own. Then, with an inarticulate groan, he swept her in his arms and held her fiercely to his chest. "Robyn, Robyn . . ." Her name was a litany of joy as he rained kisses on her cheeks, her eyelids, her hair. She was unaware of the dampness on her cheeks as bubbles of laughter spaced her own kisses. When she could stand it no longer, she stilled his face with her hands and gave him her lips.

She was only dimly aware of how they assisted each other in removing their clothes. Her body came back to life when she found herself on the bed, Philip lowering himself into her outstretched arms. They were both driven by the same overwhelming hunger sharpened by their abstinence.

They stroked each other with increasing urgency as if driven to reaffirm their memories. Her body flowered under the message conveyed by his sensitive fingers, ripening with the force of aroused passion long denied. She gloried in his adoration even as her senses sang in a renewed awakening. Would she ever get enough of inhaling the intoxicating aroma that was uniquely his, of enjoying the elixir of the slightly salty taste of his skin as she rained kisses over his neck and shoulders?

Her hands rediscovered their wonder as they molded the strong lines of muscles banding his back. She thrilled remembering the love words that now never left their throats but were unspoken avowals of sensuous delight and anticipation.

How had she existed? she wondered, before willingly drowning in the whirlpool of exquisite passion only this incredible man could evoke. Driven by the need to become one with him, she opened to him, giving into his keeping her heart, her soul, her love. . . .

Robyn's fingers moved languidly through his hair, brushing the strands from his damp forehead. His head was cushioned between her breasts and her body was purring with a deep contentment. They had so much that still needed talking over, but for now she was dreamily envisioning how her neglected family room would look turned into his work studio, Baylor once again running freely on a beach.

Philip pressed lingering kisses on the soft swell of her breast. "You can have no idea how often I dreamed of this—of having you in my arms and then resting with my head in just this position, monitoring your heartbeat. These past months, all I had to hold on to to keep my sanity were Serina's words, and I often despaired, fearing that they had come from her imagination."

"Serina?" Robyn asked in surprise.

"After you left, I spent a hellish month raging against the stacked deck life had dealt me. One day, after I snarled at something Serina had said, she let me have it. Her deductions were simple: I'd been acting like a raving maniac since you left, so it must be because of you. She told me to stop acting like an idiot and go back to you, that anyone could see how much you loved me and that you must be hurting too."

He shifted to rest his head on the pillow beside her,

and continued as his fingers brailled featherlightly over her features.

"I suddenly realized that that was part of my problem, that you had never said you loved me, and somehow her words gave me hope. As you had told me, it was my hands that created, directed by my mind, and I still had the use of both of them. Finally I accepted the new direction I had to take. But first I had to find out if I was capable. It took me all these months, and the show is the result. I made certain the invitation was sent to Cornell in desperate hope that it would bring you here."

"What if it hadn't?" she teased, kissing the pad of his finger as it passed over her lips.

He rose over her and propped himself on an elbow. "I'd have come after you. A man can hunger only so long." His mouth settled over hers, and the delightful spirals of warmth started to build in her.

"Where shall we spend our honeymoon?" he whispered, as the tip of his tongue traced with gentle persistence the intricacies of her ear.

His hand stilled when she stiffened on hearing his question and the enormity of that final commitment swept through her. She'd always been independent, not even sharing her apartment with a roommate in those earlier years when it would have been easier on her budget. But who was she fooling? For all these months she'd tried to live without this dynamic man and had found it to be an empty existence. Minutes before, she'd have accepted their living together, but he was offering more, much more. Hadn't she already envisioned his studio in her house? More importantly, hadn't she given her love into his trust?

The tension drained from her and her body softened under him. No, she wasn't a fool—she was one of the lucky ones who had found her man. Her hands smoothed the lines of anxiety from his forehead as she pressed a kiss on the corner of his mouth.

"Do you think your bure in Fiji is still livable?" she whispered against his lips.

The growl in his throat told of his pleasure as his mouth trapped hers. For a fleeting moment Robyn wished they were already on the island, tasting the happiness they'd shared there, but Philip's kisses brought her to the present. What difference did it make where they were? Rapture was being in Philip's arms, and she slid her hands over his shoulders as she joined him in its glory.

YOU'LL BE SWEPT AWAY WITH SILHOUETTE DESIRE

$1.75 each

1 ☐ James

2 ☐ Monet

3 ☐ Clay

4 ☐ Carey

5 ☐ Baker

6 ☐ Mallory

7 ☐ St. Claire

8 ☐ Dee

9 ☐ Simms

10 ☐ Smith

$1.95 each

11 ☐ James

12 ☐ Palmer

13 ☐ Wallace

14 ☐ Valley

15 ☐ Vernon

16 ☐ Major

17 ☐ Simms

18 ☐ Ross

19 ☐ James

20 ☐ Allison

21 ☐ Baker

22 ☐ Durant

23 ☐ Sunshine

24 ☐ Baxter

25 ☐ James

26 ☐ Palmer

27 ☐ Conrad

28 ☐ Lovan

29 ☐ Michelle

30 ☐ Lind

31 ☐ James

32 ☐ Clay

33 ☐ Powers

34 ☐ Milan

35 ☐ Major

36 ☐ Summers

37 ☐ James

38 ☐ Douglass

39 ☐ Monet

40 ☐ Mallory

41 ☐ St. Claire

42 ☐ Stewart

43 ☐ Simms

44 ☐ West

45 ☐ Clay

46 ☐ Chance

47 ☐ Michelle

48 ☐ Powers

49 ☐ James

50 ☐ Palmer

51 ☐ Lind

52 ☐ Morgan

53 ☐ Joyce

54 ☐ Fulford

55 ☐ James

56 ☐ Douglass

57 ☐ Michelle

58 ☐ Mallory

59 ☐ Powers

60 ☐ Dennis

61 ☐ Simms

62 ☐ Monet

63 ☐ Dee

64 ☐ Milan

65 ☐ Allison

66 ☐ Langtry

67 ☐ James

68 ☐ Browning

69 ☐ Carey

70 ☐ Victor

71 ☐ Joyce

72 ☐ Hart

73 ☐ St. Clair

74 ☐ Douglass

75 ☐ McKenna

76 ☐ Michelle

77 ☐ Lowell

78 ☐ Barber

79 ☐ Simms

80 ☐ Palmer

81 ☐ Kennedy

82 ☐ Clay

YOU'LL BE SWEPT AWAY WITH SILHOUETTE DESIRE

$1.95 each

83 ☐ Chance	95 ☐ Summers	107 ☐ Chance	119 ☐ John
84 ☐ Powers	96 ☐ Milan	108 ☐ Gladstone	120 ☐ Clay
85 ☐ James	97 ☐ James	109 ☐ Simms	121 ☐ Browning
86 ☐ Malek	98 ☐ Joyce	110 ☐ Palmer	122 ☐ Trent
87 ☐ Michelle	99 ☐ Major	111 ☐ Browning	123 ☐ Paige
88 ☐ Trevor	100 ☐ Howard	112 ☐ Nicole	124 ☐ St. George
89 ☐ Ross	101 ☐ Morgan	113 ☐ Cresswell	125 ☐ Caimi
90 ☐ Roszel	102 ☐ Palmer	114 ☐ Ross	126 ☐ Carey
91 ☐ Browning	103 ☐ James	115 ☐ James	
92 ☐ Carey	104 ☐ Chase	116 ☐ Joyce	
93 ☐ Berk	105 ☐ Blair	117 ☐ Powers	
94 ☐ Robbins	106 ☐ Michelle	118 ☐ Milan	
